Mokee Joe

RECHARGED

PETER J MURRAY

h
Hodder
Children's
Books

a division of Hodder Headline Limited

To the growing army of Mokee Joe enthusiasts . . .
always remember . . . *nowhere is safe!*

Copyright © 2004 Peter Murray
Illustrations © 2004 Simon Murray

First published in Great Britain in 2004
by Hodder Children's Books

6

A Catalogue record for this book is available from the British Library

ISBN 0 340 89296 X

Typeset in Garamond by Avon DataSet Ltd,
Bidford-on-Avon, Warwickshire

Printed and bound in Great Britain by Bookmarque Ltd, Croydon, Surrey

The paper and board used in this paperback by Hodder Children's Books
are natural recyclable products made from wood grown in sustainable forests.
The manufacturing processes conform to the environmental regulations
of the country of origin.

Hodder Children's Books
a division of Hodder Headline Limited
338 Euston Road
London NW1 3BH

www.mokeejoe.com

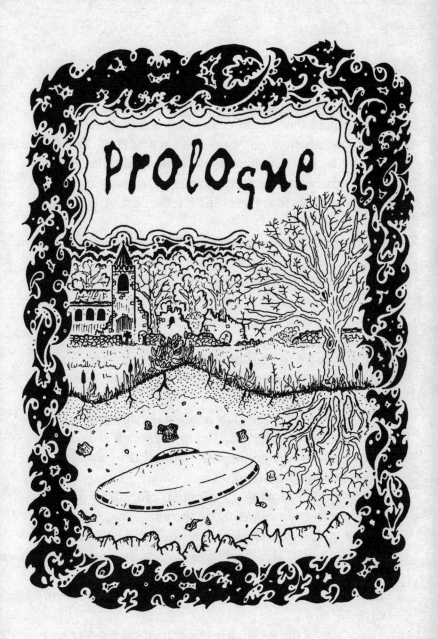

One fine February afternoon, six members of the Danvers Green Metal Detector Club visited a desolate, marshy area near to the abandoned Norman church of St Michael de Rothchilde. It was believed that a medieval village had existed there and it was hoped that someone might stumble across a few interesting artefacts or even the odd coin or two.

As it turned out, things proved far more interesting.

One of the members decided to sweep a grassy mound on the far side of the church and his detector responded in a very strange way. Further sweeping revealed an unusual expanse of hard metal extending over a large area about four metres below the surface. Several members dug down to the layer and attempts were made to break off fragments for analysis, but the material proved too hard.

The president of the club notified the authorities and scientists were called in. Using X-rays, it was soon discovered that an impressive elliptical disc lay buried below the marshy ground.

Finally, high-ranking government officials arrived at the scene and subsequently, to the amazement of those present, a strange craft was excavated and hoisted aloft by a huge crane. The object was eventually removed by lorry and taken away for further examination at a Ministry of Defence establishment near the Scottish border.

Members of the metal detector club, local services and

the press were legally bound over to keep the bizarre find quiet and undisclosed.

In the months that followed, government scientists examined the craft, holding regular meetings to discuss their findings.

Little did they realise that every move they made was being followed and recorded by a greater mind – a brain so advanced that its power was far beyond their understanding.

Outside the Ministry of Defence Special Unit, just beyond the perimeter fence, a small tent remained hidden between two grassy mounds. Inside, a man with an enlarged head, divided into four distinct lobes, sat cross-legged, staring forward with pupil-less eyes – a faint smile on his craggy face.

1

Warnings

Hudson Brown crept into the loo, pulled the plastic seat cover down and sat on it. He didn't need the loo in the physical sense, but this was one of the few places where he could almost guarantee peace and quiet – the required conditions for total focus and concentration.

Leaning forward with his forearms resting on his legs and his hands clasped together, Hudson tried to sort out the confusion of thoughts swirling around in his mind.

As he began to relax, he allowed his head to fall forward and he found himself staring down towards the skirting board. Just by the door, in a corner, he spotted a small spider clinging to its web and immediately thought of his old friend, Spiffy. This caused his mind to wander back to those sinister events that seemed such a long time ago. But in reality, it was only just over a year since that amazing night when his dreaded enemy, Mokee Joe, had been captured in the biscuit factory.

During the last twelve months his uncle and ally, Guardian Angel, or GA as Hudson liked to call him, had periodically made contact in one way or another to reassure him that Mokee Joe was still safely under lock and key. But it was six weeks since the last message and Hudson was beginning to worry.

Ever since that dreadful news about the death of his real parents, Hudson had thought of GA as his nearest, real relative – a sort of father figure; someone who really understood him – and right now on this dreary Sunday night Hudson missed him and was desperate to hear from him again.

Sitting there, in the quietness of the tiny room, Hudson decided it was time to have a go at tuning in – making contact through meditation and thought transference – something he was becoming better and better at.

He relaxed and closed his eyes fully. There was no need to stare at a candle flame any more – his powers of concentration had developed considerably and he could empty his mind almost at will.

'GA, are you there?' Hudson whispered. 'Please talk to me. I need to know that you're still around and everything is OK.'

Hudson waited, concentrated deeply – no reply.

He concentrated harder and focused his mind so intently that his inner-self entered into a void – no toilet, no clean smell of disinfectant, no spiders clinging to webs; all gone, just total blackness – waiting for that kind, familiar voice to break into his consciousness.

'GA, please speak to me. It's been such a long time. Are you there?'

A loud rapping shook the door:

'HOW LONG ARE YOU GOING TO BE IN THERE, LAD?'

Hudson jumped so violently that he fell sideways off the toilet seat and rolled on to the floor.

'Sorry, Dad . . . I think I . . .'

'. . . FELL ASLEEP AGAIN! SOME THINGS NEVER CHANGE!'

Mr Brown, Hudson's adoptive dad, ranted on outside the door until Mrs Brown came upstairs to find out what all the noise was about. Hudson deliberately delayed a little, pretending he was pulling up his trousers and tucking his shirt in. As he flushed the loo he heard Mrs Brown outside on the landing, scolding her husband and sending him away downstairs.

'Some things never do change,' Hudson chuckled to himself. And he was grateful for that. He liked Mr and Mrs Brown just the way they were. They were the best mum and dad in the world – at least in this world – even if they weren't his real parents.

As soon as the coast was clear, he crept out of the toilet and into the adjacent bathroom to wash his hands – all part of the act.

Hudson glanced at his watch and mimicked Mrs Brown's voice to himself, *'Hudson! Chocolate's ready – don't let it go cold!'* He dried his hands on the big fluffy towel as Mrs Brown's voice sounded from downstairs.

'HUDSON! CHOCOLATE'S READY. DON'T LET IT GO COLD!'

Hudson smiled and set off downstairs. He stopped

thinking about GA and felt a warm glow inside as he made his way to the cosy front room of the little terraced house.

He passed Mr Brown in the hallway looking very flustered. 'About time, lad! If ever I win the lottery, the first thing I'll treat me and Mum to is one of them bathrooms built on to the side of the bedroom.'

'*En suite*,' Hudson informed him as his adoptive father made his way rapidly upstairs.

A few moments later Hudson was sitting in front of the TV with Pugwash purring contentedly on his lap. He stroked the cat's soft fur with one hand and sipped at a mug of hot chocolate with the other. There was some sort of game show on the screen, but he wasn't really taking any notice.

'Penny for them?' Mrs Brown said as she walked in from the kitchen.

Hudson turned towards her and looked up from his mug. 'What do you mean, Mum?'

'Penny for your thoughts,' she smiled. 'It's a saying – it just means that I can see you're thinking about something.'

'Oh, I was just wondering what Molly and Ash are up to.'

Mrs Brown arranged the cushions in an armchair by Hudson's side and then sat next to him. Hudson looked at her silvery hair, tinged with a purple-blue colour – she'd spent all of the previous afternoon at the hairdressers. She smiled back at him.

'They're probably sitting quietly just like you – only they'll be wondering what *you're* up to.'

Hudson looked back to the screen. She was probably

right. The three of them did everything together – especially since the events of a year ago. Since then, they'd grown even closer. And now, somewhere deep inside himself, Hudson sensed things were about to flare up again. He *was* worrying inwardly and Mrs Brown knew it.

Pugwash jumped down from his knee and he watched as the cat sauntered over towards the gas fire and stretched out on the thick sheepskin rug.

He finished his drink, got up and moved off towards the kitchen.

'I think I'll go to bed a bit earlier tonight, Mum. I'm tired.'

Mrs Brown smiled and went over to the sideboard to get her knitting.

'OK, Hudson. God bless. Sleep tight.'

'And you, Mum.'

Before drawing the curtains in his room he instinctively looked down. The old metal dustbins had been replaced with plastic wheelie bins and their outlines stood out in the shadows. Suddenly the hairs on the back of Hudson's neck stood on end. There was nothing there – no giant lurking rat or suchlike – but Hudson felt a distinct coldness; a chill in the air that shouldn't have been there. Something was definitely wrong.

He climbed into bed, snuggled down under his duvet and took longer than usual to drift off to sleep.

Hudson's eyes flickered open. The old clock on the sitting-room sideboard sounded its chimes. He counted them nervously . . . Bong! Bong! Bong!

It was three o'clock in the morning.

Something had disturbed him. He lay there in the darkness, straining his ears for any sounds other than the ticking of the clock, but all was silent . . . or was it?

There was a different sound – a background noise, maybe, but a sound that shouldn't have been there. Hudson strained his ears so hard that he could almost hear his own heartbeat.

And then it registered. It was a distant, high-pitched whine and, like the clock chimes, it seemed to be coming from downstairs.

Hudson slipped out of bed, grabbed his rubber torch off the bedside cabinet and crept out on to the landing. Keeping his torch beam low, Hudson moved slowly down the staircase.

With every step the unnatural sound grew louder and more sinister. It was definitely coming from the front room. Hudson felt his stomach tighten.

He paused on the bottom stair. He dared not think what might be waiting around the corner. Something was wrong – very wrong.

With his heart racing, he stepped off the final stair, crept ever so slowly into the doorway of the sitting room, took a deep breath and shone his torch inside.

The TV set was on, buzzing with a snowy-white picture and making the high-pitched whine. Hudson sighed with relief, but then tensed again. His parents would never leave the set on – his mum checked everything religiously before going to bed.

He cautiously shone the torch all around the room, but could see no sign of any break-in or burglars. He focused the beam on the armchair in front of the TV and then felt compelled to go over and sit in it.

Puzzled by his own actions, he switched off the torch and sat there in the dark, staring at the screen, watching the thousands of snowy white dots hissing and crackling in front of him. And then he almost jumped out of his chair as a huge ghostly head materialised before his eyes.

'Tor-3-ergon – I see you responded to my call. Your powers of transient consciousness continue to develop.'

Hudson wasn't too sure about words like 'transient consciousness', but he sensed they had something to do with the fact that he'd been disturbed in his sleep and compelled to come down and investigate.

He took in the appearance of the familiar alien head divided into four distinct lobes. 'Hi, GA,' he replied in a nervous but friendly tone. 'It's great to see you again – I've been really worried. I've got a feeling that you're going to tell me something awful has happened.'

'That is correct. But I can do more than tell you – I can show you. Watch the screen and all will be revealed. When you know the truth, I will return.'

And saying this, the familiar head dissolved back into the snowstorm. Hudson sat forward, his hands clasped together on his lap, his hair almost touching the screen.

And then the picture re-formed; a different scene materialising before him.

Two men in uniform, one carrying a huge bunch of keys, appeared to be standing in a dimly-lit, dingy corridor. Hudson saw that they were outside a heavy metal door – some sort of prison cell. One of the guards was peering into it through a small window. As Hudson stared the picture became clearer and he could hear what the men were saying.

'Aye, it's been a whole year now and still no one's done anything.'

'The trouble is – *no one knows whit to do*,' the other guard replied in a hushed tone. 'I'm thinking the truth is everybody's scared stiff of *him* or *it* or *whatever it is*.'

The first guard nodded solemnly. 'Aye, it's the way he just sits there – never moving, never giving anything anyway. It fair makes my flesh creep.'

'Makes *your* flesh creep? Jings – what about me? You weren't driving the van that night. If the heater hadn't packed up, I'd no be standing here now. I still have nightmares about that huge clawing hand, reaching out to grab me.'

Hudson listened with fascination. It was like some TV film and it was hard to believe that this was really happening. He moved his head even closer to the screen as the picture changed again. The camera (though Hudson knew it was more than a camera) zoomed in on the heavy door and Hudson found himself peering through the small window, as if looking through the eyes of the guard.

He recoiled in horror.

There, at the back of the cell, sat the unmistakable figure of his old enemy, Mokee Joe. He was wearing the familiar grubby coat and black felt hat; sitting there cloaked in shadows, sinister and forbidding and as still as a statue. Hudson sensed the fear and dread that his enemy instilled in the guards – *and also in him*.

'How long will they keep him here?' the first guard muttered nervously to his companion as they moved on along the dark passage.

'I've heard a rumour that they're going to ship him to a

remote island, somewhere in the Outer Hebrides, and attempt to do tests and experiments on him.'

'Och – rather them than me,' the first guard sighed.

And they walked quickly away.

Hudson tensed again as the picture continued to change, moving further into the cell now, so that the frightening image of Mokee Joe drew closer. Hudson noticed that there was no blue glow – his enemy was weak, uncharged – and this was no doubt why he sat there like a statue, conserving every ounce of energy.

This thought helped Hudson relax a little – but then, as the shadowy face drew ever closer, for the first time the head moved. It turned a fraction toward Hudson's line of vision and the horrible sneering expression came into view. It was as if his enemy could see him – was aware that he was watching . . .

For the second time Hudson jumped back and his heart began to race.

And then the picture broke up again.

It was a great relief to see GA's face reappear.

'You have seen the face of our enemy?'

'Yes, I have,' Hudson acknowledged. 'But at least he still seems to be under lock and key. So what's the bad news?'

'Keep watching.'

Once more, the picture broke up and re-formed.

Now Hudson found himself looking down on to a small square yard surrounded by roofs of buildings. Something was lying on the ground and as the view dropped closer he saw that it was a bag. It was ripped open and full of white powder and the contents were blowing away in a strengthening wind.

Oh, no! It's flour! Hudson thought to himself.

It didn't take long for him to work out that he was looking down on to a prison yard and that the flour sack was lying outside a store shed. Worse still, he guessed that in some way the energising white particles were finding their way to his enemy.

As if to confirm his thoughts, the picture changed again so that Hudson now found himself at ground level, looking across the yard towards a small window with three iron bars. One of the bars was moving and bending and then all three bars were being ripped out in the haze of a bright blue light.

Hudson's jaw dropped as he realised what was happening.

The flour, most likely dropped off a lorry, was blowing into Mokee Joe's cell and rapidly recharging him.

And so it seemed that the dreaded moment had arrived – as he surely knew it would one day. His terminator was about to escape.

GA's face appeared on the screen again. 'I have more bad news . . .'

Hudson braced himself. 'Go on . . .'

'I'm afraid that I have to tell you that Mokee Joe is growing stronger.'

'I know – the flour – I saw it.'

The tone of GA's voice deepened and sounded more serious. 'No – more than that. During the creature's captivity he has not wasted his time. His electronic brain has been extremely busy, calculating how he can absorb and utilise the Earth's magnetic field. He can now raise the voltage of his body to new levels.'

Hudson tried desperately to understand what GA was saying. 'I don't really know what . . .'

'I'm sorry,' GA apologised, sensing his confusion. 'In simpler terms it means that Mokee Joe is capable of unleashing electricity of much greater intensity than before. He will not require flour or any other energy source once he is out of the cell. He only need seek out and align his circuits with magnetic lines of force and—'

'So now Mokee Joe is even more dangerous?' Hudson interrupted, rapidly realising the seriousness of what his mentor was saying.

'I'm afraid that is so,' GA replied. 'I will try to stay in contact and keep you informed of his whereabouts. In the meantime, keep the Molly girl and the Ash boy close. As before, you will need all the help—'

'WHAT THE HELL'S GOING ON?'

Hudson almost jumped out of his skin as he swivelled round to see Mr Brown standing there in his dressing gown and slippers, hands on hips and with a very stern look on his face.

Hudson's head filled with panic. How could he possibly explain being downstairs at three in the morning, and even more difficult, the image of GA, there, on the screen?

Mrs Brown appeared behind her husband, a hairnet on her head. She was also wearing her dressing gown (covered in roses) and her favourite rabbit slippers with whiskers and fluffy tails. Hudson had never really worked out why his mother – or anyone else for that matter – would want to wear rabbits on their feet.

'Come out of the way, Ernest. It's obvious the boy just couldn't sleep.'

Hudson swivelled back in fright and looked at the

screen. The picture had broken up again and he sighed inwardly with relief.

And then, to his horror, the whining started again. But this time it grew louder and more high-pitched than before. Mr and Mrs Brown put their hands over their ears and looked on with shocked expressions.

Hudson reached over to the set to switch it off and his heart missed a beat. How could he switch it off . . . *It was never switched on in the first place!* He put his fingers in his ears and tensed, focusing his eyes on the screen, willing it to stay blank.

The set screamed louder still and Hudson watched in horror as the face of his demon enemy began to form from the chaos of fuzzy dots. He stared forward, concentrated even harder, willing it to go away.

Mr Brown cursed and decided to take matters into his own hands. He moved towards the set, but before he reached it, the television screen exploded with a deafening bang, blasting a million fragments of glass all around the room.

2

Growing Pains

It was Monday morning and Hudson and Molly were sitting next to each other on the window side of a large, airy art and design studio. Several weeks into the term and the new Year 7s were busily involved in a double Art lesson at their new school, Scrubwood Comprehensive, known to its pupils as 'The Scrubs'.

'So what caused it?' Molly whispered in an excited voice.

'I think it was some sort of concentrated energy, all focused on the screen – GA, Mokee Joe and then me . . . that's the only explanation I can come up with.'

'Well, what did your mum and dad say?'

Hudson carried on speaking without looking up. He appeared heavily engrossed in sweeping a thin stick of charcoal across his picture composition. But really he was going over and over the events of the night; trying to take in GA's warning and wondering what was going to happen next. 'Not too much, thankfully. I think they were just in a state of shock. Dad said that the tube was old, but that he'd "*Never seen anything like it in all my days*",' Hudson mimicked, forcing a chuckle at the same time.

Molly giggled. 'And don't tell me – your mum went and put the kettle on and made you some hot chocolate?'

Hudson stopped sketching and glanced up at Molly's smiling face. Since she'd scraped her hair back into a ponytail he thought she looked much more grown-up.

'You're exactly right, Moll – that's just what she did. And then the vacuum cleaner came out from under the stairs and it didn't go back until every piece of glass had been sucked up. It was five o'clock in the morning before anyone got any sleep.'

'Oh, you poor thing,' Molly teased. 'It's no wonder you're looking all bleary-eyed.'

'It's not funny,' Hudson moaned, going back to his drawing again. 'This is serious. I think all my problems are about to start up again.'

'You mean *our* problems.' Molly sounded more sympathetic. 'Remember, we're all in this together – the three of us. It'll be like old times.'

Hudson looked back at her. 'I suppose we ought to have one of our meetings in Candleshed – then it really will be like old times. Shall we meet at seven tonight?'

'OK.' Molly nodded as she spoke. 'We'll see Ash later and arrange it.'

Hudson picked up a pencil and started drawing a star in one of the top corners of his night sky. But as he tried to concentrate, the horrible vision of Mokee Joe's escape invaded his mind, opening the floodgates to a sequence of depressing thoughts:

He's out there again . . . and he's coming to get me . . . and my father made him . . . blaming me for my mother's death . . . just because I happened to be born . . . as if it was anything to do with me . . .

Hudson shuddered – and then his pencil snapped.

The strength that he had suddenly gained more than a year ago, just prior to his final battles with Mokee Joe, had stayed with him and he'd learnt to control it. But now he was growing even stronger and it was proving very difficult to live with this 'new power' and to keep it hidden.

Miss Drew, the Scrubs Art teacher, came over to Hudson's side. 'Oh, Hudson! You must have pressed too hard. Never mind, go and get another pencil off my desk.'

Hudson returned a minute later with a new HB pencil, sat at his table and continued with his drawing.

A short while later another cracking sound resounded through the room. 'Oh, I'm sick of this!' Hudson muttered under his breath.

Miss Drew, who was now seated back at her desk, looked up. 'Oh, Hudson! Don't tell me you've broken another one?'

The whole class stopped and stared at him. He couldn't help thinking that lots of the pupils who had come from other primary schools were staring at his odd, hot-cross-bun hairstyle and thought him rather strange. This made him feel uncomfortable and he looked to Molly for reassurance.

But Molly could only giggle as Miss Drew came over,

carrying an entire container of new pencils. She placed it on Hudson's desk. 'There you are, dear. That should keep you going to the end of the lesson.'

Everyone burst out laughing and Hudson felt himself blush.

Molly leaned over and whispered in his ear, 'And if you break all those, dear, you can use mine!'

Hudson gave her a friendly nudge and picked up another pencil. He tried to keep calm and took extra care not to break it. He couldn't bear the thought of attracting any more attention.

The Scrubs dining hall was much bigger than the one the three friends had grown used to back at Danvers Green Primary. Consequently, the noise level was much higher and Hudson found himself almost shouting across the table at Ash.

'So don't be late – seven o'clock at my place.'

Ash looked up from his rapidly disappearing plate of chips and beans. 'No worries – I'll be there. It'll be like old times.' And then Ash's face changed from a smile to a frown as the reality of what he'd just said sank in.

Molly patted him on the head. 'Don't get too worried – we'll be there, right beside you. It's only a meeting.'

Hudson wasn't hungry – too much on his mind. He put his cutlery down, sat back and brushed his hands through his hair so that it flattened and then sprang back even higher than before. He had an idea. But as he picked up his knife and fork again he realised that he'd bent them out of shape.

Hudson hoped Molly and Ash hadn't noticed and continued quickly. 'It might only be a meeting, but I'm going to try and contact GA. Do you remember that time in Candleshed last year?'

Molly started peeling an orange. She deliberately dropped a piece of peel on to Ash's plate to annoy him and Hudson chuckled.

But Ash was beginning to look really nervous and never even noticed. 'You mean with the paper and pencil – writing down messages and suchlike? I don't know, Hudson. If you ask me—'

'Well nobody *is* asking you!' Molly interrupted, dropping another piece of peel on to the edge of his plate. 'If you can't hack it then you really don't need to be there.'

Hudson looked at Ash to gauge his reaction. Molly was right. The old trio could only work together if they were all up for it – there could be no half measures.

'Of course I'll be there,' Ash said as convincingly as possible. 'You know I will.'

Hudson looked at Molly and she looked back at him. They both knew that Ash meant it – he would be there and it really would be like old times.

And yet in other ways Hudson knew that things would be different. Hadn't GA warned him that his enemy was now more dangerous than before?

He looked at his two friends and felt guilty. It was his problem and he really didn't have the right to involve them. Perhaps he ought to disappear and take his problems with him – away from Danvers Green, away from his loving adoptive parents and his good friends.

Ash suddenly shrieked out and spluttered.

Molly started laughing uncontrollably and passed him a glass of water.

It seemed Ash had just swallowed a piece of orange peel.

Hudson laughed and felt comforted again. He knew that he and Molly and Ash had a very special relationship, one that no one could break – not even the demon Mokee Joe. With GA's help, there was a very real chance he could fulfil his destiny and overcome his enemy once and for all.

He began cutting up a sausage with renewed determination – and then the fork handle broke in half. Molly looked at Ash, Ash looked at Molly, and they burst out laughing.

It was five minutes to six and Hudson sat in his usual place with Pugwash curled up on his knee. He stared at the place where the TV had been. There would be no six o'clock news tonight!

Mr Brown walked in and sat in his favourite armchair and stared at the same empty space.

'I've never seen the likes of it in all my born days,' he muttered without looking at Hudson. 'The worst of it is I'll miss my gardening programme now. It's so blooming annoying.'

Mrs Brown walked in. She looked at Hudson's face, looked at her husband's stern expression and tutted in disapproval. 'I don't know! First night without a telly and you two look like a pair of lost sheep.'

She walked over to the sideboard, switched the radio on and returned to the kitchen to fetch the tea.

Music blared out for a moment and then a voice declared: *'It's six o'clock and it's time for the latest news headlines.'*

Hudson stroked Pugwash and found himself half listening. Mr Brown picked up a newspaper and turned to the back page to read the sport.

'Police have reported the escape of a dangerous prisoner from a maximum security unit in the Scottish Highlands.'

Hudson tensed so much that Pugwash jumped down from his knee.

'Police are asking people living in the vicinity to watch for anyone behaving suspiciously. They are insisting that no one should approach the man under any circumstances.'

'Blooming ridiculous!' Mr Brown suddenly blurted out to nobody in particular.

Hudson looked over at him and saw that he was still engrossed in the newspaper.

'Five million pounds they paid for him and he can't even score a goal. They'd 've been better off giving the money to charity.'

Mrs Brown walked in carrying a tray of tea and biscuits. She put the tray down on a small table at the side of her husband and passed the plate of biscuits over to Hudson.

'Police are unable to give an accurate description of the fugitive at the moment; only to say that he is exceptionally tall and wearing clothes similar to those of a vagrant – grubby coat and a black hat. Any information should be phoned through to . . .'

Hudson almost yelled out and dropped the plate on to the floor. The biscuits broke, sending fragments and crumbs all over the swirly-patterned carpet.

'I think this house is cursed!' Mr Brown snapped, putting his paper down and staring at Hudson. 'Are you all right, lad?'

Mrs Brown looked at Hudson sympathetically. 'You do seem a bit jumpy lately. Is there anything you need to tell us?'

Hudson leaned over the arm of his chair, started picking up the broken biscuits and avoided any eye contact. He hated telling untruths to his parents. 'No – everything's fine. I'm just a bit tired. I'm still getting used to the new school.'

Mrs Brown went over to the stairs to get the vacuum cleaner again.

Mr Brown got up and stood in front of the fire. Hudson watched with interest as his adoptive father placed his thumbs inside his braces and looked up towards the ceiling. As he was about to speak he stood on Pugwash's tail so that the cat wailed and went out of the room in disgust. There was no doubt that a speech of a serious nature was about to be delivered.

'Now look 'ere, son. We all remember what happened a year ago and we're never likely to forget it. You did us proud and no one can deny it. And as far as we know, the evil beggar that caused all the trouble is well out of the way . . .'

Hudson sighed inwardly. *If only that were true*. But at least he was sure now that Mr Brown hadn't heard the radio announcement. And he was sure Mum hadn't either. And this was just the way he wanted it. He didn't want either of them worrying about anything just yet. Best to keep them out of it.

'. . . and you know you only have to ask and me and Mum will do our best to protect you, son. Do you see what I'm saying?'

Hudson nodded.

Speech delivered, Mr Brown sat down and went back to his paper.

Mrs Brown returned with the vacuum cleaner and just as she was about to say something, there was a knock on the door. Hudson jumped up and went to answer it.

It was Ash.

He stood there on the doorstep looking as white as a sheet and shaking like a leaf. 'Hudson . . . I don't suppose you saw the news—'

Hudson cut Ash short and shouted over his shoulder. 'Just going down to Candleshed, Mum! When Moll arrives, send her out to us.'

And saying this, he grabbed Ash's arm and marched him off down the garden to prepare for the meeting in which they both sensed anything might happen.

3

Memories

'Hudson, this shed really could do with a bit of a tidy-up. I guess you're just too busy in here with your telescope to notice.'

Hudson glanced across at Molly. She was staring at him, elbows planted firmly on the old wooden table, head cradled in her hands. He knew that behind that casual look of concern she was secretly thinking about more recent events and worrying for him. She was trying to cheer him up – take his mind off things and keep a sense of normality. He knew he was lucky to have such a good friend.

He looked around the old shed. It smelt a little fusty and there were more cobwebs around the windows and in the corners than he'd ever seen. There was a dampness in the atmosphere and a feeling of neglect. But then again – they'd hardly ever bothered to meet here after Mokee Joe's capture.

Since Hudson had got really interested in astronomy, he'd used the old shed as a sort of amateur observatory, never really bothering about how clean and tidy it looked. Once or twice, Mr and Mrs Brown had commented on the amount of time he'd spent in there gazing up at the planets and making notes.

'It's not natural for a young lad to be spending so much time in an old shed,' Mr Brown had muttered more than once so that Hudson could hear.

Of course, Mrs Brown always defended him. 'Leave him be, Ernest! Hudson's a bright boy and needs hobbies and such to keep his mind busy. No harm will come of it.'

'Never mind tidying up,' Ash butted in, bringing Hudson swiftly back to the present. 'What about the news? Did you see it? I'm sure they were talking about Mokee Joe. He's escaped.'

'Yes, I saw it – well at least I heard it,' Hudson replied. 'You're right, Moll, this shed does need a good clean out, but there's more serious matters to think about at the moment – like how long before Mokee Joe arrives back in Danvers Green?'

Molly said nothing. She got up, looked around and found an old red candle. It was starting to get dark. She took the matchbox off the table – Hudson had placed it there earlier – and lit a match. As she lit the candle the shadows began to flicker around the grimy walls.

Ash went very quiet and Hudson sensed his anxiety.

'We could certainly do with an update,' Hudson said

in his most serious voice. 'Did you bring the pen and paper, Moll?'

Molly placed the red candle in the centre of the table and reached down into her bag. Ash began to rub his hands together nervously. She passed a small pad of paper and a Biro over to Hudson and then sat down with her arms folded across the table.

'OK. Here goes, and no one panic. Ash . . . are you OK?'

Ash fidgeted in his chair. 'Don't worry about me – I'll be fine.'

Hudson took a final look at Molly to check she was of a similar mind, but he knew he had no worries there. He peered over her shoulder to the cracked mirror still adorning the wall by the door. Memories flooded back. 'Turn that mirror round to face the wall, Moll. I don't want any distractions.'

Without question, Molly did as he asked and everyone braced themselves as Hudson began to stare into space and focus his mind. He held the pen firmly over the paper and prepared to write.

The atmosphere began to feel different.

The air went heavy and the shadows grew deeper and flickered around the walls with more menace. Everything outside seemed to go very quiet, as if the night itself was holding its breath in anticipation of what might happen.

Ash began to shake so much that the table began to rattle. Molly reached over and grabbed one of his wrists and held it tight.

Hudson stood and stared, his head facing the shed door, but he saw nothing. His hand trembled a little but it refused to write.

'It's not working,' Ash whispered across to Molly.

'Sshhh . . . give him time,' she replied.

Hudson felt his body go as still as a stone statue. His pupils grew smaller and rolled back so that his two anxious friends could see the whites of his eyes.

But, as before, nothing happened. No words scribbled on the pad. Nothing!

All sorts of weird images flooded into Hudson's mind, beyond his control – whirling patterns of light and colour and pictures beginning to form that made no sense to him. He knew that GA was tuning in and was about to take over.

And then two light beams shot from Hudson's eyes straight over Molly and Ash's shoulders.

They swung round and gasped in amazement.

There on the shed wall, the two beams focused and formed a blurry image – like a projector on a cinema screen.

'Moll, look!' Ash uttered in disbelief.

As Ash and Molly watched, a picture formed. It showed a convoy of vehicles driving down a long straight road. The view was from above – like a bird's eye view.

'What is it?' Molly whispered. 'What are we looking at?'

'I don't know, but look, there's someone running by the side of the road. Can you see the top of his head – by that middle lorry?'

Molly nodded in surprise. 'Yes – what does it mean? It must be important – it's got to be a message from GA.'

Ash looked at Hudson, who was standing there as if carved out of stone, the intense beams of light continuing to shine from each of his eyes. And then he looked back to the shed wall. The lorries were still there, travelling ever onwards, but the chasing figure by the side of the road had gone.

The light dimmed again and the image disappeared.

Ash and Molly quickly turned to look back at Hudson. His eyes, though still staring forward, had otherwise gone back to normal.

His body began to shake and now he felt his hand move towards the paper. There was no panic. He wasn't exactly sure what was happening, but he knew who was guiding him and it was reassuring to feel GA's presence.

A few seconds later, without ever looking down, Hudson became vaguely aware of the rasping sound of his writing hand scribbling over the paper's surface . . . slowly at first, but gradually increasing in speed . . . and then, just like the last time, the candle went out and all was in darkness.

But no one panicked – not even Ash – nor did he make a run for it. To Molly's amazement, it was he who rooted around for the matches and shakily relit the candle.

When the light returned, Hudson was slumped back in his chair looking exhausted.

'Did anything happen?' he asked his two friends in a weary but excited tone of voice.

'You bet it did,' Molly replied. 'You half scared us to death.'

Hudson gathered his senses and Ash and Molly took it in turns to tell him all the goings on. It was only when the full tale had been told that anyone remembered to look at the pad of paper.

They studied it at the same time, and then gazed at each other in complete bewilderment – nothing made any sense. Hudson had scribbled two groups of jumbled letters on the paper, one on the left and the other on the right.

YU EEY IL RIE N TAN   OR NM WL ARV I A RI

Hudson looked straight at Ash. Molly looked straight at Ash. Ash continued to stare at the letters and then looked back at his two friends. 'Sorry, I haven't a clue,' he said sheepishly. 'But don't worry – I won't rest 'til I've cracked it.'

Hudson sat on the end of his bed and reached over for the small resin block sitting on the top of his dressing table. He held it in one hand and stroked it affectionately with the other. Maybe he would show it to Molly and Ash tomorrow, though he knew they would be upset to see the dead body of Spiffy preserved inside – especially Molly; she would really be upset. But it was good of Mr Millbank to provide him with the preserved body of his friend.

When Hudson had taken the lifeless spider to the Scrubs Science teacher, Mr Millbank had explained that house spiders only live for around one year. He'd kindly immersed the dead arachnid in a dish of clear liquid resin and provided Hudson with a permanent reminder of his companion.

'Don't worry, Spiffy,' Hudson whispered. 'I know you're still with us in one way or another. I'll be keeping you close to me – you're still just as much a part of this battle as the rest of us.'

And saying this, he gave it another gentle stroke and then put it under his pillow.

Before going to bed, he switched on his PC and logged on to e-mail. As expected, there was something from Ash. He clicked on it and waited in excited anticipation.

Hudson

GA must really be having communication problems but I finally cracked it! It took ages. If you take the letters on the right and then mix them alternately with the letters on the left, it all makes sense – well sort of. It spells out . . .

YOUR ENEMY WILL ARRIVE IN A TRAIN

I suppose the convoy of lorries must be something to do with MJ on his way here and maybe he was the figure running by the side of the lorry . . . but why would GA say he's arriving in a train? And in any case, shouldn't it be ON a train?

See you tomorrow.

Ash

Hudson sighed inwardly. Ash was bright, there was no doubt about that. Only he would have cracked the strange lettering so quickly, but even Ash was baffled by the nature of the message. What could it mean?

Hudson got up and paced around his bedroom, his head full of confused thoughts.

Pugwash suddenly walked in purring. Hudson picked him up and sat on the edge of his bed stroking him, trying to think what to do next. Still holding the cat he got up again and looked out of the window. The moon was bright and as he stared at it he sensed that something was not quite right. He would need to take a closer look through his telescope tomorrow night.

With all these thoughts going through his head, he placed Pugwash gently on the window ledge, watched him jump down on to the roof of the kitchen extension, checked that there was nobody suspicious moving about among the black, shadowy wheely bins, and finally got into bed and fell into a restless sleep.

Hudson couldn't quite make out what it was he was sitting in – a kind of rickety old carriage, but with an open top. Everything was black around him – and yet he knew that he was hurtling along a bumpy track.

Some sort of metal rail pressed against his stomach and he gripped it with both hands to stop himself from falling out.

It was so scary: careering on into the darkness, not knowing where he was or where he was going. And then he saw a huge grinning skull illuminated in front of him. Worse still, he seemed to be heading straight towards it. Only at the very last second did the carriage veer away and as Hudson looked back over his shoulder it disappeared back into the darkness.

Hudson held on, his heart beating ever faster as more terrifying images looked set to bar his way. Dancing skeletons, witches with grotesque faces, dangling hairy spiders . . . all disappearing as magically as they appeared, and always at the last moment, just as Hudson felt sure he was going to crash into them.

As he lurched around another corner and almost fell out of the carriage the smell of diesel oil filled his nostrils. Everything was pitch black again – he couldn't even see his hand in front of his nose. And then a loud siren screamed out making him jump in his seat. He clung on tighter as the carriage accelerated – *faster, faster, faster*.

The siren screamed even louder – like a warning – and then Hudson looked ahead and saw his worst nightmare; lit up in electric blue like a fluorescent phantom, standing there with its arms outstretched towards him, evil and menacing.

It was Mokee Joe.

As the carriage picked up even more speed, the demonic figure of his enemy loomed before him. Now Hudson could see the grubby coat and felt hat quite clearly.

He braced himself, sure that his seat would veer away from the terrifying image, and lurch around a sharp bend, as it had already done so many times before.

But to Hudson's horror, Mokee Joe just kept on drawing closer – and now Hudson was only a few metres away. And then the horrific face was upon him – evil, staring, bloodshot eyes, ragged nose and grinning fangs . . .

BANG!

Everything came to a shuddering halt. Mokee Joe had been rammed – full on.

There was a horrible smell of burning paint and diesel oil, and the sound of hissing steam and grinding metal.

But Mokee Joe never flinched. He just stood there, towering above the shocked Hudson, grinning and reaching down.

Hudson felt the huge, cold hands grab him around the neck and lift him from the tangled metal, forcing him to look into those haunting eyes. He felt the knobbly fingers tighten around his throat and begin to squeeze the life out of him.

And then intense pain as bolts of blue electricity shot through his body.

The face moved closer, the mouth dripping some sort of oily saliva, drooling and moving closer still, ready to take a lethal bite . . . and then Hudson screamed.

At first the scream wouldn't come out. It stayed in his throat – there was no noise at all, just muffled darkness all around. He screamed again and again, forcing himself back, pulling at the life-draining hands – but this time the scream did ring out, echoing around the black chamber.

He tried to reach down into his pockets for Spiffy, but he wasn't there, he was where Hudson had left him, under his pillow.

He screamed for Molly and Ash, but they were nowhere to be seen either. How could they be? He didn't even know where he was himself.

And so with a desperate feeling of frustration Hudson screamed just one more time – a scream so loud that even his own ears hurt as a result.

'*Hudson! Wake up! You're having a nightmare.*'

He stirred and opened his eyes. Mrs Brown was sitting on his bed, by his side. She was looking down at him, smiling softly, but her eyes were full of concern.

'Are you OK, Hudson? You were making a horrible din – you almost woke Dad!'

'Sorry,' was all he could think to say.

'No need for that,' Mrs Brown said sympathetically. 'No one can help having nightmares. Why don't you sit up and I'll get you a drink? Try thinking about some nice things before you go back to sleep – and then you'll have sweet dreams.'

And so while Mrs Brown went to get Hudson a drink, he sat up and thought about Molly and Ash and Pugwash . . . And then he couldn't help thinking about that horrible dream. It was more than a dream – much more than a nightmare. He just knew there was a message in there somewhere – a warning, maybe.

Mrs Brown returned.

He talked to her quietly whilst sipping the cool, clear water and felt more at ease. And finally, as Mrs Brown turned out the light, he lay back on his pillow, and sure enough he fell into a peaceful sleep . . . dreamy and content . . . *Until the same nightmare started all over again!*

4

Rivals

Hudson, Molly and Ash stood huddled together in the playground. It was drizzling and cold.

Molly tugged at Hudson's arm. 'You look really tired. Did the nightmares eventually stop?'

Hudson nodded his head and looked at her. A raindrop splashed off his hair on to her nose and he laughed as she jumped back and wiped it off with her coat sleeve.

'Yes, eventually – but I don't want a night like that again.'

'You can bet your life somebody was trying to tell you something,' Ash joined in.

'I know – but I just can't work it out. What do you make of it?'

Ash put his hands deep into his pockets and looked

down at the ground. Hudson saw the thoughtful look in his stance. 'Dark tunnels and scary things jumping out at you – and then Mokee Joe standing there. I can't think what it means except—'

'Hi there, Hudson,' a different voice suddenly butted in.

'Hi, Karen,' Hudson replied shyly, looking over Ash's shoulder.

Karen Blott, like them, was one of the new Year 7s, but had come from a different primary school on the other side of Danvers Green. She had already shown herself to be extremely nosy and was always around if she suspected any interesting gossip was taking place. She was standing behind them with two friends.

'How's things?' Karen continued, smiling straight at him, mouth chewing gum at the same time.

'Well, we're just—'

'. . . having a private conversation!' Molly finished the sentence for him.

Hudson felt awkward. Karen frowned at Molly.

'Nobody was speaking to you,' Karen said coldly, her two friends nodding in approval and also glaring at Molly.

'No – and nobody asked you to stroll over and crash into . . .'

But before the argument could develop any further, the school bell rang out and everyone moved off. Hudson sighed inwardly. Ash looked at him and smiled.

Hudson thought that there were enough complications in his life right now without his friends bickering and falling out. He sighed and quickened his pace towards the school entrance.

* * *

Hudson and Ash trotted out on to the fields without speaking. Neither of them liked Games and the thought of spending an hour out in the cold and wet failed to fill them with much enthusiasm.

Something else that Hudson disliked about Games was that he really wasn't sure about the Games teacher. There weren't many adults he had misgivings about, but here was a man who wasn't to be fully trusted. Hudson eyed him suspiciously.

'OK then, let's have you all seated by the touchline. I want everyone watching carefully as I demonstrate how to kick a ball – it's not as easy as you might think.'

Mr Fotheringill was a typical Games teacher – a big, broad-shouldered man with a wide chest and a square head capped with short, curly hair. A firm jaw and tight mouth gave him a look of no nonsense and determination.

The Year 7s watched with interest as the Games teacher walked on to the pitch, placed a greasy wet football on the penalty spot and stepped back.

The voice of Mr Fotheringill boomed out again. 'Now as you approach the ball you must keep well balanced. As you bring your foot down, strike it with the side of your foot – not your toe – allowing your kicking leg to follow through so that you achieve maximum force.'

And saying this, the Games teacher ran up and kicked the ball sweetly into the centre of the empty net.

The Year 7s applauded and Mr Fotheringill turned to face them, looking very pleased with himself.

'But, sir,' a feeble voice suddenly shouted out, 'the goal was empty.'

Hudson and most of the other Year 7 boys swung

round to see who had been brave enough to challenge the proud man in front of them. It was Bertie Small.

Hudson knew it wasn't bravery – it was definitely stupidity.

Mr Fotheringill walked over, put his hands on his hips and leaned forward towards the cowering form of his challenger. 'Well then, Small . . . I'll tell you what we'll do. We'll put a keeper in the net and I'll have another go. How about that?'

'Good idea, sir,' Small answered nervously.

'Well, what are you waiting for? GET IN THERE!'

Hudson felt really sorry for Small as he made his way over to the net and took up a position on the goal line.

Ash came across to Hudson and crouched next to him. 'This Fotheringill guy's a real bully, Hudson – what do you think?'

Hudson nodded and then winced as the teacher ran up and kicked the ball with tremendous force. The Year 7s watched in awe as the ball rocketed towards the unwilling goalkeeper. It smacked into Small's palms, bending them backwards and knocking him over. The ball finished up in the corner of the net.

Hudson and Ash watched sympathetically as Bertie Small went back to his place on the touchline, rubbing his hands together, almost in tears, and looking thoroughly wretched.

'I don't think there was any need for that,' Hudson muttered to Ash, looking over at the smug expression on the PE teacher's face.

Ash suddenly changed the subject. 'Hudson, I was trying to tell you earlier in the playground. I've been thinking about your dream again – it seems to me that you were on some sort of ghost train.'

Hudson had never actually been on a ghost train, but as Ash described one to him he could only agree that it seemed to fit his nightmare experience.

'But where does Mokee Joe come into it?' Hudson said thoughtfully. 'Ash, I'm getting really worried. We need to know his whereabouts – it won't take long for him to get down to Danvers Green and—'

'YOU TWO! GET OVER HERE!'

The Games teacher had spotted them deep in whispered conversation. They got up sulkily and sauntered on to the pitch.

'I won't even ask why you two were chatting away instead of concentrating on the matter in hand. Well, now it's your turn. And let's just say that if you don't make a good attempt at kicking this ball you are going to find yourself on a very long run around these school fields. Do I make myself clear?'

Hudson and Ash looked up at the big, glowering face and nodded solemnly.

'And we'd better have a goalkeeper or young Small there may get upset again – so I'll go in goal. OK with you, Small?'

Over on the touchline Bertie Small nodded pathetically, still close to tears.

Ash took his shot first. It wasn't a very strong kick and it almost trickled up to the waiting hands of the gloating teacher.

'Is that the best you can do, lad? If Hudson doesn't do any better you'll both be off on that run – you need toughening up.'

Most of the other Year 7s chuckled and waited in eager

anticipation to see what would happen next. Hudson prepared himself and took a few steps back whilst Ash replaced the ball on the penalty spot.

'Go for it, Hudson,' Ash whispered to him. 'We don't want to do that run, do we?'

Hudson most definitely did not want to do that run. In Hudson's world, the only time for running was when you were being chased. 'I'll do my best,' he whispered back.

As Hudson prepared to take his shot, the Year 7 girls appeared. They were carrying hockey sticks and were obviously on their way back to the changing rooms. Quite a few of them stopped, curious to see how Hudson would fare in his attempt to score against the athletic Mr Fotheringill. Molly gave him a wave, which greatly embarrassed him.

'Get on with it, Hudson – we haven't got all day!'

Hudson readied himself and ran towards the ball. But just as his foot was about to strike it a cheer rang out from the crowd of spectators and distracted him. He missed the ball completely, spun off balance and fell over.

Half of the Year 7s burst out laughing. The other half were still cheering and looking over to the right of the school field as a convoy of lorries and caravans cruised past on its way to the common.

'Hooray – it's the fair! Brilliant!' somebody shouted.

Molly ignored them and looked over to Hudson. She felt really sorry for him.

'NEVER MIND THE FAIR,' the PE teacher bellowed. 'Keep your eyes on me or you'll all be joining young Hudson and Ash on their cross-country run . . .'

'But, sir,' Hudson shouted, 'I was distracted. Just give me one more chance, sir.'

The Games teacher sneered back at him, 'OK – but if you miss this time, you'll both run twice the distance.'

'But, but . . .' Ash complained.

'NO BUTS – GET ON WITH IT!'

The convoy of fairground vehicles disappeared so that the road was empty again.

Now all eyes were on Hudson as he teed the ball up for the second time.

Hudson felt sorry for Ash. He felt sorry for Bertie Small. In fact he felt sorry for anyone who had to put up with the bully standing there in front of him. It was definitely time to show old Fotheringill that he wasn't the only one with a bit of strength and ball control, just because he was older and bigger.

Stepping back one last time, Hudson focused his undivided attention on the ball sitting on the penalty spot. As he concentrated, he felt his heart pumping faster and the blood surging into his leg muscles. He felt the energy of something deep inside channelling itself into readiness to strike the ball – and then, as Ash and the crowd of spectators held their breath, he ran towards it.

As Hudson's right foot struck the greasy wet ball it exploded with a deafening bang. At the same time, it compressed into a flattened discus shape and took off faster than the human eye could see towards the startled goalkeeper. Mr Fotheringill ducked instinctively and his quick reaction saved his life. He was fortunate only to feel the lethal missile shave the top of his head and scorch a track through his hairline. The entire crowd, including Hudson, watched open-mouthed as the flattened ball tore through the back of the net and soared away into the distance.

In a complete state of shock, Mr Fotheringill slowly straightened up and walked over to the Year 7s. Without speaking, he pointed them back to the changing rooms. Hudson and Ash quietly shook each other's hands and followed, Molly running up to join them.

As they left the school field Hudson was aware of the Games teacher staring at him in disbelief and watching his every move. He never said a word, just stood there, gawping. Hudson noticed he was also shaking a little.

The other Year 7s ran up and congratulated Hudson and wanted to know how he'd done it – especially Scott Masters, captain of the football team.

'It was just a fluke,' Hudson kept saying. 'The ball must have been pumped up too hard – that's all I can think of.'

Most of the crowd seemed to accept his explanation, but he could see that some of them were not convinced. Bertie Small looked at him suspiciously, and Karen Blott and her two mates just stared.

Molly and Ash simply laughed. They knew their friend was different if no one else did, and Hudson was glad they did – because with true friends he knew that he need have no secrets, and right now, Molly and Ash were the best friends he could have in the entire world.

He turned to them and smiled.

'You're looking really pleased with yourself, Hudson,' Molly said, tugging at the sleeve of his football shirt.

'I'm not surprised after showing that bully what for,' Ash added.

'That fair going past,' Hudson replied, modestly changing the subject. 'Do you fancy giving it a go on Saturday night?'

'I'm sure we're both up for it if you are,' Molly answered for the two of them.

Ash nodded.

And then, before they could say anything else, Hudson trotted off and they followed him towards the warmth of the changing rooms.

That night, before going to bed, Hudson slipped down to the garden with his torch and went into Candleshed. It was a full moon and an opportunity not to be missed.

Some minutes later, Hudson swung his telescope round, looked into the clear night sky and focused on the huge bright orb. He scribbled notes and looked again – and then he scribbled more notes. His suspicions were correct – something very strange was happening up there. He would need to monitor the situation very closely because he believed that in some strange way it was all connected to what was happening to him down here.

He decided to take a final look, but a line of cloud moved across the moon and everything turned a shade darker. A few isolated raindrops were already beginning to fall. It was time to call the astronomical proceedings to a halt.

Half an hour later he was back in the house, sitting in the front room, cradling a football in his lap. Mr and Mrs Brown had bought it for him the previous Christmas.

Mr Brown peered over his newspaper, 'A bad choice that present,' he said sternly. 'You've never really been interested in sport, have you, lad? That ball – it looks brand new.'

Hudson stared at the shiny plastic. It looked brand new because he'd never used it. It had stayed in his bedroom, under the bed. But now, after the Fotheringill incident, he'd suddenly felt compelled to bring it down and examine it. He had no idea how he had managed to kick that ball so hard during Games and had been just as shocked as everyone else.

He spun the black and white ball around in his hands – like a revolving planet.

'Dad . . . did you know that the pattern on this ball is made up of twenty hexagons and twelve pentagons?'

Mr Brown lowered his paper and looked across. 'Is that right, son?'

'Yes – and altogether there are one hundred and eighty interior angles giving a total angle sum of twenty thousand eight hundred and eighty degrees.'

Mr Brown lowered his paper further. His eyes narrowed and he looked at Hudson in a very strange way. 'Fascinating, lad. Fascinating.'

Hudson said nothing else. His father went back to his newspaper.

Of course, what's really fascinating, Hudson thought to himself, almost shaking with excitement, *is that it's only taken me a few seconds to work that out in my head*.

Hudson yawned and walked into his bedroom. The rain, heavier now, made a tapping sound on the window. The bedroom curtains hadn't been drawn properly – there was a gap and Hudson decided to close them fully, to shut out the unwelcome night. As he approached he saw the condensation trickling down the glass and noticed that the vapour had formed patterns. For some reason he felt compelled to look up towards the top of the pane, and as he did so, his heart thumped.

The letters were quite clear, like someone had drawn them with an index finger, the sort of thing you do on a school bus on a steamed-up window.

There were only two words, but they were enough for Hudson to get the message and cause the butterflies to invade his stomach. He took a last look, reached up and rubbed out the words, and yanked the curtains closed.

Later that night, lying in bed, he concentrated on everything good that had happened during the day. But no matter how hard he tried, he couldn't get that message out of his head. The tighter he closed his eyes, the clearer he saw those two words standing out on the steamed-up window:

HE'S ARRIVED!

5

All the Fun of the Fair

Hudson, Molly and Ash stood at the entrance to the fairground.

It was Saturday night and the fair was in full swing. Their hearts began to beat faster as the smell of diesel oil, mingled with hot dogs, onions, doughnuts and candyfloss, filled their nostrils. The noise was deafening. They stared in awe at the huge rides lit up with thousands of brightly-coloured bulbs, which mirrored the twinkling stars high in the clear night sky.

To Hudson, it was a truly amazing spectacle.

'Hudson, have you had any more thoughts about GA's coded message?' Ash asked, gazing around.

'No. Last night I got another message.'

'More codes to crack?' Ash asked, sounding excited at the prospect of another challenge.

'Not this time – this was as clear as crystal!'

Hudson told his two friends about the message on the window pane, and then Ash told Molly how he'd cracked the earlier message.

'So first, Mokee Joe's coming on a train, or "in" a train, and now it seems "he's arrived" already. It all sounds a bit crazy to me.'

Hudson couldn't disagree. He nodded solemnly.

'But if he's arrived . . . then where is he?' Ash suddenly asked in a very shaky voice.

At first, Hudson said nothing. He felt a headache coming on, and this was unusual for him. The fact that he had hardly slept lately hadn't helped. He took a few steps forward and stared straight ahead before answering, 'I don't know. Let's just enjoy ourselves and try to forget the scary stuff for a bit.'

'Sounds good to me,' Ash replied in a cheerier voice.

Molly came up by his side. 'Are you sure you're OK, Hudson?' She was wearing her faded denim jacket with a silver star on the breast pocket. Hudson loved it. She smiled up at him and he noticed for the first time that she had some small silver discs hanging from her ears.

'Moll, you're wearing earrings,' he uttered in surprise.

'My mum let me buy them. Definitely not to be worn at school, only on special occasions – like when I'm out with friends and stuff.'

Ash leaned over and peered at them with a curious look on his face, as if he'd spotted something.

'Hey, what are you doing?' Molly cried out, pushing him away.

Hudson was surprised to see Molly react like this, she looked flustered.

'There's a letter or something stamped on one of them – I think it's an "M",' Ash declared.

'M for Molly – what's wrong with that?' she demanded, stroking her earrings and pretending to look hurt.

'And what about the other one?' Ash teased. 'S for Stevens, I suppose.'

'That's for me to know and you to find out,' she laughed, half looking at Ash and half looking at Hudson.

Hudson laughed with her. And then he blushed a little. He knew exactly what the other earring had stamped on it.

'Come on! Let's go and have some fun,' he said cheerfully.

But inwardly, he was beginning to feel very frightened. He should have had more than enough clues from GA now to know what was going to happen next, but he and Ash had failed to put all the pieces together. It was something to do with a train . . . but what? And now he was getting a bad headache.

As the three friends walked on, Hudson prayed that they really would enjoy themselves and that the next stage of the battle wasn't waiting around the corner.

Molly put her arm through his and pulled him out of his trance. 'Come on! I want to show you something.'

The trio moved deeper into the noisy crowd, and eventually wandered up to the side of a small, brightly-coloured kiosk. Big letters proclaimed the name of the owner – MADAME ZAZA.

'What's this?' Hudson asked as Molly dragged him closer.

Ash answered for her. 'A gypsy fortune-teller. Moll wants to find out if you two are gonna get hitched one day.'

'Oh shut up, Ash – don't be stupid.' Molly suddenly let go of Hudson's arm. 'I just wanted to know if we're all going to survive this Mokee Joe thing – I thought it might be good to hear what she has to say.'

Hudson stared at the notices painted on the sides of the kiosk, all from customers praising Madam Zaza's mystical powers.

'You don't really believe all this stuff, do you, Moll?' Ash asked as he scrutinised the colourful posters.

But before Molly could say anything, the door of the wooden kiosk opened and out came a woman whose appearance instantly intrigued Hudson.

'Can I tempt you to come in and learn your fortune?' she asked, scanning all three of them – but her eyes rested immediately on Hudson's strange, hot-cross-bun hairstyle.

Hudson took in her bright gypsy robes and the silk headscarf covered in red and white dots, tied in a knot around the back of her head. But it was her face that proved the most interesting.

It was an old face, in fact it was so wrinkled it could have been over a hundred years old. The nose was large and bent – like on a pirate mask – and the eyes were small, black and piercing – rather too much like another pair of eyes he knew. On one of her cheeks she had a huge spot – like a boil or a wart. It intrigued Hudson so much he couldn't stop staring.

'Go on, Hudson, have a go, just for me – I'll pay half.'

'No, Moll – it's still too expensive. Five pounds is a lot of money – even when split.'

'Well I'll put in a third,' Ash piped up. 'I really would like to see this. It'll be worth every penny.'

Hudson didn't want to let his friends down. He looked at the woman again. There was something he didn't trust about her. At the same time he was curious to hear what she had to say, so reluctantly he agreed and the three of them followed the strange old gypsy into the dimly-lit kiosk.

Inside, it was spooky and dark. A single red light focused down on to a big, circular table with an impressive crystal ball placed at the centre. The air was smoky from some sort of incense burning in a dark corner; all in all Hudson felt quite at home and began to relax.

The old gypsy sat down. She invited Hudson to sit opposite her and gestured to Molly and Ash to sit on either side.

Hudson watched with interest as she reached out and placed her hands over the glass ball. At the same time she closed her eyes and seemed to go into some sort of trance. She began speaking as if she was getting a message from some invisible source.

'Ah . . . something is telling me that you are a boy with purpose . . . on a mission of some kind . . .'

The three friends almost jumped out of their seats with surprise. Did she really know all about Mokee Joe and Hudson's purpose on Earth?

'Ah . . . I have it . . . You are determined to ride the biggest rides in the fairground . . . to test your courage, perhaps?'

Hudson smiled at Molly and Ash. So that's all she meant. He leaned over and whispered, 'She probably says that to every kid who comes in here, because it's probably true – they all want to go on the biggest rides . . .'

The gypsy heard Hudson's whispering and opened one of her eyes – she looked at him suspiciously.

'Will he grow up and get married and stuff like that?' Molly asked the old woman in an excited voice.

The gypsy opened both her eyes, leaned forward and gazed intently into the glass ball.

'Indeed, the ball is misty tonight . . . it's having great problems telling me about this young man . . . he appears to be shrouded in a cloak of mystery.'

'Well, I think you're right about that,' Ash chuckled. 'There's no one more mysterious than Hudson.'

Hudson spoke next. 'Can you tell me anything about any danger or threat?' he asked in a very serious voice.

He watched as she looked up from the crystal ball. She began to stare at him in a very strange way. He noted that she seemed very interested in his hair again.

'I need more time . . . the forces are weak and you are surrounded by an intense aura of energy. I'm having trouble getting through.'

She paused, and then, without any warning, Hudson placed both his hands flat on the table and stared back. In fact, he stared so hard at the woman that she let go of the crystal ball and almost fell back off her chair.

He continued to stare without blinking, focusing easily on the mind behind the old gypsy face. 'Your real name is Alice Cricklewood. You joined the fair when you were fourteen – when your mum and dad split up. You ran a coconut shy for ten years and then took up fortune-telling.'

The old woman gasped. 'I knew you were a strange

one. How do you know these things?'

Molly and Ash looked on in surprise. Hudson turned to Molly and smiled.

'That's for me to know and you to find out,' he said, looking back at the old, wizened face. 'I also know that the spots and most of the wrinkles are just make-up. You're only thirty-nine – in fact, forty next month.'

Hudson started to get up. Molly and Ash did the same.

'I think you'd better give us our money back,' Molly said, her face beginning to turn into a scowl, 'that's if you don't want everyone in the fairground to know you're a fake.'

The woman stood up and banged a five-pound note down on the table so that the crystal ball fell over, revealing a sticky label on the bottom.

The three friends leaned over and read it – *Made in Taiwan* – then they burst out laughing. The woman grew even angrier and went red in the face.

As they were pushing back out through the door, the fortune-teller grabbed hold of Hudson's arm and spun him round.

'Just one thing before you go,' she said in a half-angry, half-determined voice. 'Whatever you think, I do take my job seriously and I *can* tell fortunes – *sometimes*. Not everybody's as difficult as you – but I'll tell you one thing for sure: I know that you're a very special young man and that a great problem awaits you.'

Molly and Ash swung back round.

'What do you mean?' Ash challenged her. 'Why are you trying to scare him like that?'

Hudson could see by Ash's frightened expression that *he* was the one who was really scared.

'Oh, the young man knows exactly what I mean – after all, he knows everything, doesn't he? There's something very wrong and it's just waiting around the corner – something evil . . .'

Hudson looked into the woman's eyes and this time he knew that she was speaking the truth – she saw the danger that confronted him.

'I'm sorry we were rude,' he said meekly. 'I know that you do have some special power – it's just that silly disguise . . .'

The gypsy woman calmed down. 'Purely for the customers, dear – it's what they want to see, what they expect.'

Hudson apologised again and beckoned to his two friends. As they walked out into the noise and bright lights, Hudson looked back and saw the gypsy standing in the doorway. She was staring at him, her face full of sympathy. Hudson turned away feeling more anxious than at any other time. His headache was now ten times worse – a real pulsating pain – and he was beginning to feel sick.

'Hudson, what was all that about?' Molly asked, her voice full of concern. 'Could she really see some sort of danger – something around the corner and all that?'

Hudson didn't reply.

He walked on like a zombie, his heart beating faster – on through the crowd, past a huge rocket ride, screams from its occupants filling his ears. Molly and Ash had a job to keep up with his big strides.

'Hudson, what's wrong?' Ash demanded in a shaky voice.

Molly grabbed Hudson's arm and clung on. 'Where are you taking us?'

But still Hudson didn't answer.

Taking even bigger strides, Hudson marched on past the dodgems towards the noise of a high-pitched siren sounding in the distance. Finally, much to Molly and Ash's relief, he stopped. He put his head in his hands, pulled his hands back through his hair and looked up and pointed.

Molly and Ash looked in front and gulped together.

There was the source of Hudson's anxiety.

As Ash and Molly stared, the penny finally dropped so that now all three of them knew exactly where the enemy was – where Mokee Joe was hiding – right there in front of them . . . *inside the ghost train*.

6

'Of course! It all makes sense!' Ash cried out as they moved slowly towards the ghost train.

Hudson was very quiet.

Still walking on, Ash continued, 'That business in Candleshed—'

'With the lorries, and the chasing figure?' Molly interrupted.

'Yes – it was the fair, on its way here – lorries and caravans and things.'

Hudson still said nothing. He walked on, staring straight ahead, only half listening to the ongoing conversation.

'And then there was Hudson's dream – the dark tunnel and those ghostly things – and then Mokee Joe . . .'

'It *was* a ghost train, wasn't it?' Molly said, chewing on her thumbnail.

Hudson finally joined in. 'That was the message that GA tried to get through to me – about the train – only I never thought of a *ghost* train.'

He turned – looked first at Ash and then at Molly. His expression was deadpan and serious. 'He's in there and that gypsy woman sensed the danger – somewhere nearby – a place like this.'

He turned back and faced the huge ghost train – ghoulish decorations adorning the wood panelling, muffled screams echoing from inside, the sound of a siren. 'I should have realised earlier. That day the convoy went past the sports field something didn't feel right. Old Fotheringill put me off with his bullyboy tactics.'

The thought that Mokee Joe had been so close at that particular time sent a shiver down Hudson's spine.

Molly clung tightly to one of his arms, in a supportive way. Ash clung just as tightly to the other.

Molly tugged at his sleeve. 'Is that monster really in there?' she asked in a determined voice.

Hudson stared forward, his gaze penetrating straight through a garishly-painted vampire standing at least four metres tall.

'He is. I can feel his presence – he's in there all right!' he answered, rubbing his head. 'And the headache – I've got a horrible feeling I know what's causing it.'

'Go on . . .' Molly asked, hardly able to contain her curiosity.

'Mokee Joe is trying to get into my head – read my thoughtwaves – I'm sure that's the reason.'

Ash nervously scanned a huge painted skeleton

dressed in a station porter's uniform. It was wearing a peaked cap and waving a green flag at a painted phantom express. 'Do you mean he knows you're here?'

'Probably.'

'If he is in there, Hudson, shouldn't we stop people from going inside?' Molly asked.

As she spoke, Hudson watched two girls climb into one of the train carriages and pay their money to an old man with some sort of money satchel attached to his waist. One of the girls was taller than the other and looked familiar.

'Oh my God – Hudson, I don't believe it,' Molly suddenly gasped, pointing at the two girls. 'That's Karen Blott and Sandra Hickson.'

Hudson reacted instantly. He jerked his arms free and ran towards them waving and shouting. 'STOP! KAREN – GET OUT!'

A loud pop tune blared out from a nearby ride and what with the roar of generators and all the other fairground noises, Hudson's warnings were drowned out.

In desperation, he made straight for a small flight of wooden steps leading up to the carriages, but it was too late. A spooky siren screamed out and he could only watch helplessly as the train carrying the two girls lurched forward and banged through two saloon-type doors, each decorated with an ominous grinning skull.

The last thing Hudson saw was Sandra hiding her face behind her hands and Karen laughing loudly.

As Ash and Molly ran up and joined him, a second train crashed back into the fresh air from the doors behind them.

They all swung round and watched in amazement as a

young boy almost fell out of the train, crying hysterically. His father jumped out of the other side in a fit of temper and made a beeline for the man taking the money.

'You blithering idiot!' the boy's father screamed at the startled money taker. 'You'll give somebody a heart attack.'

'Are you mad or something?' the man replied. 'What the devil are you going on about?'

'That monster in there! Running around and putting the fear of God into my son – and me for that matter – I've never seen anything so terrifying! It should be X-rated if you ask me. I've a good mind to report you to the council. I'll get this thing shut down – you see if I don't!'

Hudson, Molly and Ash watched open-mouthed as the man grabbed his blubbering son and dragged him down the steps and away into the crowd.

'Hudson – what shall we do?' Molly asked, fists clenched and ready for action. 'We've got to help Karen and Sandra.'

Without another word, Hudson leapt up the steps, took a deep breath and readied himself to charge through the doors – but he was too late.

Molly screamed, Ash shrieked out and the man taking the money gasped as Karen and Sandra's train came hurtling backwards out of the doors, the two girls clinging to each other and wailing in terror as the demonic figure of Mokee Joe pushed them with great strength back into the cold night air.

In the next second all the action seemed to freeze as Hudson took stock of the situation.

Everybody was screaming hysterically, staring in disbelief at Mokee Joe, glowing electric blue, the monster's eyes full of menace and firmly fixed on one thing – *Hudson Brown*!

This was the moment Hudson had dreaded, and yet he knew it was only a matter of time before it happened – before the eternal battle recommenced. He knew it, GA knew it and Mokee Joe knew it.

But right now, GA didn't seem to be on hand. The only thing in Hudson's head was a throbbing pain. He needed to act on his own and there wasn't a second to lose. Mokee Joe was about to strike and had never looked stronger.

Hudson leapt down from the staging and dashed towards his two friends. 'MOLLY – ASH! FOLLOW ME! WE'VE GOT TO GET OUT OF HERE AND LURE THE MONSTER AWAY!'

They did not need telling twice.

Hudson ran into the crowd and the two friends followed. They hardly dared turn and look back for fear of what they would see chasing them.

On – on – through the crowd – bumping and banging into people. They heard the occasional scream, but lots of people were screaming anyway – enjoying the rides. But Hudson was sure the monster was on their tail – he could smell him, oily and dank – somewhere close behind.

Suddenly, the dodgems appeared in front of them and Hudson instinctively ran across the shiny floor, weaving in and out of the swerving cars. Molly and Ash followed suit, but Ash wasn't quick enough and a car veered into his path and knocked him to the ground.

'Hudson! Ash is down,' Molly yelled. 'We've got to help him!'

And so they stopped and turned. And then, to their

horror, they saw that Mokee Joe had reached the far side of the dodgems and was about to make a run towards them. More than a few onlookers saw the seven-foot demon standing there and jumped back in shock, but most people laughed and feigned horror, thinking it was all part of some fairground attraction.

Hudson and Molly dragged Ash to his feet as the man in charge of the dodgems ran over to have a go at them.

'What the hell do you think you're up to?'

No one had time to answer.

The three friends looked past him and froze with terror as Mokee Joe charged. But luck was on their side. One of the dodgems sped across the floor right into their attacker's path so that the monster stopped and grabbed hold of the metal pole reaching from the back of the car up to the power supply in the roof. A spark of electricity shot down the pole into the demon's gangly arm and his blue glow pulsed brighter. The monster looked up, distracted by the small bolts of blue charge shooting all around the roof from the cars below.

That second's hesitation was all that Hudson needed. 'Quick, run for it – make for the entrance.'

And in that same second, Mokee Joe straightened up his seven-foot frame, reached up and touched the highly-charged wire grid above his head.

The result was an almighty bang followed by a strange silence as the entire fairground plunged into darkness. Every light went out and every piece of machinery ground to a halt.

Hudson, Molly and Ash stared in a state of shock at the glowing, blue figure – it was all they could see; everything else was in blackness.

'Quick! Run!' Hudson yelled again.

They clung on to each other and dived into the darkness, the electric-blue demon charging after them.

It was Molly's turn to go sprawling next. She tripped and fell headlong on to the muddy ground.

Hudson grabbed her with all his strength and picked her up. He almost tucked her under his arm. 'Keep running . . . but don't look back. He's gaining – I can hear him.'

Ash was clinging desperately to Hudson's jacket, tripping and stumbling and almost pulling him to the ground.

Hudson sped on through the shadows, leading his two friends down the narrow gaps between the fairground stalls, turning corners, swerving one way and then veering off another – anything to shake off their fearsome pursuer.

Feeling as if he'd done one of Fotheringill's infamous cross-country runs, Hudson finally stopped and looked over his shoulder to see that the terrifying blue glow was no longer in sight. They seemed to have lost him. They crouched down in the shadows alongside the silhouetted shape of a small building.

'Stay quiet. I think we've shaken him off – but I don't know for how long,' Hudson said, breathing heavily.

The three friends crouched and listened as chaos and panic continued to sweep through the fairground. Hundreds of people were stranded in rides, some high up in the clear night sky. The only consolation was that the moon was bright and full and eyes were slowly becoming accustomed to the dark.

'What happened back there?' Molly whispered.

'GA told me recently that Mokee Joe has grown stronger,' Hudson whispered. 'He somehow made all the power short circuit and caused everything to switch off.'

'Where is he? Can he still find us?' Ash asked in a shaky voice.

'Of course he can,' Hudson replied. 'He'll be looking for us with his infra-red vision and judging by the pounding in my head he's still trying to tap into my thoughts.'

'Well for God's sake, concentrate and try to shut them out,' Molly and Ash said together.

Hudson sensed the panic welling up in them. 'We've got to get out of here,' he said in a determined voice.

'But which way?' Molly asked. 'We might bump straight into him.'

Before Hudson had time to reply, the power returned and all the lights came back on. Rides swung back into action and the sound of cheering echoed around the fairground.

Hudson shielded his eyes from the brightness; at the same time a hand slapped down on his shoulder and gripped it tightly. He shrieked out and fell backwards.

'It's OK. It's me. Quick – this way!' It was the gypsy woman. They were crouched down by the side of her kiosk. 'You need to get away from here and I can help you.'

Hudson looked up at her. The make-up had been removed. Now she looked her real age and altogether much friendlier than before. 'But why . . . ?'

'There is no time for explanation . . . I have seen the tall one with the strange blue aura. He is close by, skulking amongst the caravans like a giant rat, and waiting.'

'How do you know?' Molly asked, eyeing the woman suspiciously.

But it was Hudson who answered. 'Trust her – do as she says.'

'Let's get the hell out of here,' Ash said, impatiently.

And so the woman led them away.

It was obvious she knew every inch of the fairground. She took them on a complex route in between rides, down narrow openings, through dimly-lit shadowy places – ideal haunts for Mokee Joe – but it seemed she knew exactly what she was doing. After reaching a lonely fence on the edge of the fairground and following it for a tense five or ten minutes they stepped out of the shadows into the brightly-lit entrance.

The three friends thanked her quickly and Hudson reached into his pocket and offered her the five-pound note back, but she wouldn't take it.

'Go – go now and never come back here. The fair will be gone in a few days' time and I have no doubt the devil creature will move on too. The police are already here, asking questions and searching around. He will not stay among us.'

'You're right,' Hudson said sadly. 'He'll stay here in Danvers Green. I'm his prime target and now he's found me . . . Well, you'd never understand.'

'I understand more than you think, young man. Now go – as quickly as you can.'

Without another word, the three friends turned and set off at a trot. They jogged all the way home – panting for breath; no one speaking; constantly looking over their shoulders.

As they neared home, Hudson realised that his

headache had disappeared. It seemed that the monster wasn't in his head any more. For the moment they were safe.

But it would only be a matter of time before the next round of the battle took place and he would need more than a few headache pills to help him overcome his newly-charged enemy – *an enemy that could put out the power supply of an entire fairground with one touch of his evil hand*!

7

chalk & cheese

Monday morning, following the fairground incidents, Hudson, Molly and Ash made their way into the school assembly hall with the rest of Years 7, 8 and 9. They met up with Karen and Sandra and had a brief chat – all the talk centred on the big power cut at the fair and the seven-foot madman that had rushed out of the ghost train and caused chaos.

Hudson found himself trying to play things down by offering alternative theories to the truth. 'I heard it was some sort of crazy advertising stunt and that the man who owned the ghost train put him up to it,' he said, looking coyly at Molly and Ash as he spoke.

Karen folded her arms across her chest and snarled, 'Well if you ask me, that madman should be locked up and the key thrown away – me and Sandra nearly wet ourselves!'

Hudson looked at Ash and smiled – Molly grimaced.

A stern voice suddenly boomed out at them, 'Come on, you lot. Stop gossiping and get to your places.' It was Mr Buglass, the headteacher, or Buggles, as the pupils knew him. Mr Buglass was a large, round, pompous sort of man and not at all popular with the pupils. He stood at the centre of the stage, a younger teacher by his side, waiting for the pupils to file in and take their seats.

It was quite normal to see Buggles waiting there, ready to take Lower School Assembly, but there was considerable intrigue as to why his opposite was standing by his side. Buggles rarely allowed the younger teachers to appear on stage – he considered them a threat to his power and authority – especially the ever-popular Mr Gladstone!

'Come along! Come along!' Buggles snapped impatiently. 'Don't take all day!'

'That's a nice greeting to start the week!' Ash muttered very quietly under his breath as he filed past; but his voice carried up to the stage.

'Did you say something, young man?' Buggles asked in a very threatening way.

'No, sir, I was just saying that it's nice to have a meeting at the start of the week.'

'Just as well!' Buggles said. 'Just as well!'

When everyone was in place and settled down, Buggles tapped the microphone and began his speech. But as his mouth uttered a string of words, a corresponding whistling, whining noise issued from the mike.

It was a most weird and wonderful sound and everyone started giggling – all except Hudson.

Buggles stopped abruptly and tapped the microphone. He ordered Mr Gladstone to come over and help him and after the two of them had fiddled around with the mike and made some adjustments, Buggles tried again.

It crackled and whined louder than ever and the school laughed out loud, which angered and frustrated the headteacher so that his face took on a deep crimson colour and beads of sweat formed on his bald head.

But Hudson wasn't laughing. He was scanning around and looking thoughtful.

Ash wondered why his friend wasn't joining in with the hilarity. 'Hey, Hudson, what's wrong?' he whispered. 'Have you lost your sense of humour?'

'Yeah, what's wrong, Hudson?' Molly chipped in. 'Isn't it great seeing old Buggles squirming up there?'

'Yes, I know! But I can sense something isn't quite right. There's something sinister happening here – I can feel it.'

Molly and Ash had heard Hudson make comments like this before and they knew that it usually spelt trouble. Ash stopped laughing and began to look a little nervous.

Finally the microphone seemed to start working and the headteacher began again.

At either side of the stage on which the headteacher and Mr Gladstone were standing, a huge glass window stretched from the floor up to the ceiling. At the very top of the window on the right, just below the roof, unseen by everyone – even Hudson – something was clamped to the glass.

It was a head! In fact it was no ordinary head, it was

Mokee Joe's head, with one of his ears clamped to the glass, like a snail sticking to the side of a fish tank.

Hudson's enemy was tuning in to the radio waves emitted from the microphone and causing the interference. And now that the monster's electronic receptors were correctly adjusted the interference had stopped.

Mokee Joe could hear every word that the headteacher was saying!

'Now that we have that little problem sorted,' the headteacher started at last, 'I would like to tell you that before we have our usual hymn and short prayer, I have an announcement to make.' Buggles looked smug and continued in a cheerful tone.

'On Thursday morning, we are intending to hold the Annual Lower School Cross-country Run – that is to say, for Years 7, 8 and 9.'

A gasp of horror and disbelief issued from the new Year 7s – moans from the Year 8s and 9s.

The headteacher ignored them and continued, 'The run will take place at 2pm and the route will go out beyond Danvers Green, up by Macalisters Biscuit Factory, before returning along the towpath of the canal. A scenic and inspiring run,' he added with a smile. He looked at the sea of glum faces before him and quickly moved on.

'Well, before our hymn, "Onward Christian Soldiers", Mr Gladstone has an announcement of his own to make, so I'll hand you over to him – Mr Gladstone . . .'

The young teacher walked over to the mike looking cool and relaxed and the pupils all sat up and looked interested.

Mr Gladstone's first name was Bryn and this gave rise to his nickname of 'Brinnie'. Unlike Buggles, Brinnie was extremely popular and regarded as one of the coolest teachers at the Scrubs. Anything he said just had to be worth listening to.

'OK, guys,' Brinnie started as the headteacher winced, 'just a quick notice, but one that I think you're gonna like the sound of. As Chairman of the School Resources Committee, I'm intending to hold a fund-raising activity in two weeks' time – *a special party*.'

Everyone cheered up and looked full of expectation.

Brinnie continued, 'As the 31st October falls on a Saturday this year, I'd like to hold a Hallowe'en disco party here in this assembly hall and you're all invited. We'll charge a small entrance fee and we'll use the money to supply the IT department with some much-needed new software. What do you say?'

A loud cheer rang around the hall, greatly upsetting Buggles, who fidgeted anxiously in his chair.

'OK, you guys,' Brinnie went on, 'I'm going to suggest that we encourage fancy dress and that we have a dance-mime competition. We'll throw in a few prizes to make it more interesting. Watch the notice boards for further info; and in the meantime, start thinking what you're going to wear and start practising your dance routines, 'cos we're going to have one cool night. If you have any suggestions or anything you want to ask, I'll be only too pleased to see you.' And saying this, he left the stage.

As the Scrubs lower school sang 'Onward Christian Soldiers' Mokee Joe slid away from his prying position, completely undetected.

Hudson, still sensing that something untoward had happened, tried to cheer himself up by scanning a few minds. Was it intuition – or was he really getting better at reading people's thoughts? He couldn't be absolutely sure.

He looked round at Karen Blott. She seemed to be thinking about a very special dress that she'd seen last Saturday downtown. He tried to see the dress in his mind, but it was no good – no image would come.

He turned his attention to Molly.

She was wondering what she could wear that would really make her stand out among the crowd. Again, no image would form. Hudson would just have to wait to find out.

Finally, he turned towards Ash.

He was thinking what it could be that had been worrying Hudson. His mind seemed to be flowing with sinister images of Mokee Joe.

And this caused Hudson to go back to his own thoughts; and these too were full of his enemy – Mokee Joe, Mokee Joe; always Mokee Joe! He felt this demon would haunt him for ever . . .

8

Tense Meetings

Monday evening found the three friends in Candleshed, each reclining in a comfy chair, sipping from cans of Coke and chatting about recent events.

Hudson had given the place a good tidy-up and he noticed Molly looking around and smiling in appreciation. It pleased him to see her so happy and distracted from the real reason for them being there.

He'd even managed to persuade Mr Brown to move his few remaining garden tools out of Candleshed up to the brick store by the back door.

'I don't know what it's coming to,' Hudson had heard Mr Brown muttering to his wife. 'The next thing you know they'll be wanting to move their beds in there and install central heating and hot and cold running water!'

Hudson almost laughed out loud at the thought of it, but as his mind snapped back to the present he kept his face very straight. This Monday evening meeting was not a laughing matter – no time for jokes or any other distractions.

It was dark outside and the myriad of candles burned brightly, forcing back the gloom and giving out a wonderful aroma that helped everyone to relax a little.

Ash suddenly said, 'Why have you called us here, Hudson?'

'It's obvious why we're here,' Molly answered impatiently. 'Because trouble's brewing up.' There was a noticeable tone of excitement in her voice.

'She's right,' Hudson confirmed.

Ash looked nervous. He unwrapped a stick of chewing gum and shoved it in his mouth. 'I still can't believe he's back. The nightmare's starting all over again. Who'd have thought he'd turn up at the fair like that – in the ghost train of all places?'

'Well at least we know now what GA meant when he said Mokee Joe would arrive *in* a train,' Molly said.

Hudson scratched his chin and nodded thoughtfully with that strange look in his eyes that they had all come to dread. 'I don't know what happened after we'd left but that creature is more clever and cunning than we'll ever know and he'll never rest until he, or we, are totally defeated!'

'Any more messages from Guardian Angel?' Molly asked, squeezing her empty Coke can so that it made a loud crunching noise.

'No – I'm afraid not.'

Molly looked at Hudson. 'So we've no idea where and when the next strike will be?'

'Let's hope he doesn't get to know about the school run,' Ash added thoughtfully. 'Remember the route goes—'

'Right past the biscuit factory!' Hudson interrupted. He clenched his fist and banged it on the table, making Ash jump. 'That would be so convenient. I wouldn't put it past him to be there . . .'

'You're right,' Ash added, his voice beginning to tremble. 'There'll be over two hundred kids in that race.'

Molly rolled her scrunched-up can nervously between her hands. 'Perhaps we need to get some sort of warning out to them – just in case.'

A sudden gust of wind howled from outside and several of the candles flickered from a draught that sneaked in from somewhere.

The atmosphere abruptly changed.

The air in the shed went cold and even the tidied-up surroundings couldn't keep out the eerie spookiness that seemed to creep in on them.

No one spoke – Ash and Molly immediately looked to Hudson's face. Sure enough, he was staring straight ahead, his eyes glazing over, his mind a million miles away. And then he spoke:

'He may well turn up, but it's *me* he wants. I'm never going to have a life of my own with the two of us walking on the same planet. If the authorities capture him again, it will just be a matter of time before he makes another escape. I've got to find a way to destroy him.'

Hudson sounded desperate and the others started to feel sorry for him – especially Molly. She reached over and patted his arm. 'Was that you or GA speaking?' she asked softly.

'I'm not sure,' Hudson replied, looking goggle-eyed. 'I think it might have been a bit of both of us. But believe me,' he continued, 'I don't need GA to tell me that it's all going to come to a head before much longer. There'll soon be another showdown – and this time I'll have to destroy Mokee Joe once and for all!'

'But how soon?' Ash asked, already dreading the thought of Thursday's run.

Molly reached over again and grabbed Hudson's wrist. 'Whenever and wherever, we'll be there for you, Hudson. You can be sure of that!'

But Hudson wasn't listening. He was looking back into space as a second gust of wind, stronger than the first, rattled the windows of Candleshed and caused every single candle to flicker.

As Hudson began to speak in a shaky, spooky voice, Ash's eyes opened so wide that Molly thought he looked like a goldfish!

'This is definitely Guardian Angel telling me that the big battle for me will be at Mokee Joe's convenience – a special occasion – and that's as much as he can say.'

Molly and Ash looked serious, each desperately trying to think of other possibilities for a showdown.

Before anyone could come up with a suggestion, the shed door blew open with a mighty bang and all the candles blew out. Something heavy came hurtling through the door, landed on Hudson's lap and knocked him off his chair.

Ash screamed. Molly half yelled and half screamed. Hudson told them not to panic. It was Pugwash.

But something outside had frightened him.

Molly quickly calmed herself and relit several of the

candles. Ash was already halfway up the garden path and running for his life.

'What was all that about?' Molly whispered, feeling a little foolish that she'd screamed out a few seconds earlier.

Hudson picked up Pugwash and walked over to the open door and looked out. The cat hissed and his fur stood on end. He struggled out of Hudson's arms, jumped down and ran to the back of the shed.

'He's out there,' Hudson said in his most serious voice. 'He's out there now, close by and probably tuning in as we speak. I'm getting a headache again. He's most likely trying to read my mind. We really must start locking this door – not that it would do much good!'

Molly went over and picked up Pugwash, quickly blew the candles out and joined Hudson outside. She stroked the cat reassuringly and watched as Hudson locked the shed. Then the two of them walked nervously back up to the house and found Ash hiding by the brick store shed.

A few seconds later, the door opened and Mrs Brown stood there with a puzzled expression. She could see the troubled look on each of their faces. 'Come on, you lot. Let's have you inside. You look like you've seen a ghost.'

Five minutes later, Hudson, Molly and Ash sat around a warm fire sipping from their mugs – Pugwash purring on Molly's knee. No one spoke. Everyone was deep in thought.

And then Ash suddenly started talking about Hudson's amazing football incident and how Mr Fotheringill had never quite been the same. Hudson looked slightly embarrassed at the mention of it.

'I do seem to be getting stronger,' Hudson whispered

in a modest tone, 'though I think that was just a fluke with the football – I haven't managed to do it again.'

Molly smiled at him.

'Oh, come on! Don't be so modest,' Ash grinned. 'That was some kick. You're a special guy. We all know that. The Scrubs kids are beginning to think that you're some kind of superhero,' he went on.

Hudson felt himself blushing as he realised Molly was staring at him, her huge brown eyes blazing in the firelight. And then he found himself reading her mind.

Hudson, I'm so worried about you . . . she was thinking. *Really worried!*

9

Midnight Encounter

On the stroke of midnight Hudson sat bolt upright in bed.

His hair bristled back and stood on end. Goosebumps spread all over his icy cold skin.

There, at the foot of his bed, his dreaded enemy, Mokee Joe, stood and stared.

Hudson had never seen the creature look so terrifying.

Black, piercing eyes cutting into him like razor blades, thin lips drawn tight over drooling fangs, long bony fingers clenched into angry fists, standing there, looming, surrounded by an eerie blue glow.

Hudson began to panic as he became aware of a second shape over to his right, standing in the shadows. It spoke in a familiar reassuring voice:

'Don't worry too much, Hudson. It's not entirely real. It's a mental projection.'

Hudson recognised the voice of Guardian Angel.

'What do you mean?' Hudson asked, looking nervously back to the figure still standing at the foot of his bed.

Guardian Angel floated out of the shadows and hovered above the floor. 'Look straight into my face and then look beyond. Tell me what you see.'

Hudson was reluctant to turn away from his enemy, but he did as he was told and stared into the face of his Guardian Uncle. And then he realised he could see straight through him – to the bedroom door which was still firmly closed. It quickly dawned on him that the floating figure was semi-transparent.

'You're not real either,' Hudson gasped.

'I am real, but only in the mental sense. My physical self is elsewhere. And it's the same for the creature in front of you. His physical body lurks in a different place. Now look behind you.'

Hudson looked down at his pillow and almost died from shock.

He was still lying there – asleep. And then he held his hands in front of his face and realised that he could see through them. Like the other two, the 'sitting-up-in-bed-Hudson' wasn't real. His mind turned somersaults as he desperately tried to make sense of it all.

Guardian Angel sensed Hudson's confusion. 'Don't worry – this is not the first time your physical and mental states have become separated.'

Hudson nodded. He remembered clearly his journey to the bathroom ceiling over a year ago, and his even stranger trip over the rooftops to Kiln Street.

Suddenly, the apparition at the foot of his bed glowed more brightly. It began to glide towards him.

'Focus your mind and tell him that you are not afraid and that you are stronger than he is,' Guardian Angel instructed.

Hudson felt his body straining to move away from the fearsome sight as it reached out to grab him, but his real body was still asleep and refused to wake. And then he allowed his other self to drift up to the ceiling just in time to escape the clutching fingers.

The Mokee Joe spectre reached up after him, its face set in a terrifying grimace. Though Hudson had every confidence in his Guardian Uncle, it was difficult to believe that the demon couldn't harm him.

He willed himself to race all over the bedroom with the spectre of Mokee Joe chasing him, and for the next few minutes it all became a bizarre game.

But Hudson's confidence increased rapidly. He began to feel in control of the situation. He moved around the room with lightning speed, laughing and shrieking, dodging and diving – even teasing the ghostly phantom as Guardian Angel watched, impressed, from within the shadows.

And then Mokee Joe was gone. Disappeared in a flash of electric blue light.

The strange head of his Guardian Uncle moved once more out of the shadows and spoke to Hudson.

'You are fast becoming a formidable opponent for the evil one. Well done, Tor-3-ergon.'

Hudson found it difficult to respond to his real name. He sat back down on the bed, directly over his sleeping body.

'Guardian Uncle – please tell me more about Mokee Joe.'

'Very well.' Guardian Angel moved closer and drifted over the end of Hudson's bed. 'Your father and I designed him. He is the very latest in advanced electronic community aids – a fully automated educational assistant.'

'You mean, a sort of teacher?'

'Yes. Mokee Joe is one of many such creatures designed to carry out helpful tasks throughout the Alcatron community. Some help in schools, some are vehicle mechanics – they have many different roles.'

'So is he a robot?'

'Much more! He is a synthetic creature with skin tissue as advanced as any human. His circuitry is so sophisticated that he can think for himself and learn from experience. Because of this, his chances of survival in order to carry out the tasks as set by his programmer are greatly increased – *in this case, to terrorise children and, above all, to destroy you.*'

'And the programmer was my *father* . . .' Hudson added sadly.

He thought back to their previous conversation at Kiln Street. How could his father have possibly blamed him for his mother's death?

'I'm afraid so. He hoped that by having a child of his own, his dislike of children might be dispelled . . . that the bullying he endured as a child might in some way be compensated . . . but when your mother died giving birth to you . . .'

'That was the last straw . . .' Hudson sadly interrupted.

'Yes. I'm afraid that his reaction was completely

irrational. Your father was a brilliant robotic engineer and an expert in cybernetics. He implanted his hatred for children into Mokee Joe's circuitry so that the creature would be driven by his obsession for revenge. As soon as we discovered what he had done, the Alcatron Security Forces were alerted, but Mokee Joe was already causing havoc in the school he'd been dispatched to.'

'So why wasn't Mokee Joe arrested – taken back into captivity and reprogrammed?'

'That was the intention, but your father had made too good a job. The creature was always one step ahead – as it is now – stalking and hiding and waiting for the right moment.'

'So it escaped?'

'In a space pod – into Alcatron orbit. At first we thought the monster had trapped itself. All we had to do was blast it into deep space and it would be gone for ever.'

Hudson felt himself becoming more and more curious. 'So what went wrong?'

'A statistical error.'

Hudson knew exactly where the story was leading. 'You mean the chances of the ship arriving here – on a planet inhabited by children . . .'

'. . . are approximately twenty-five million billion to one. Exactly right,' Guardian Angel confirmed. 'But it happened. And that's why we're both here now. To rid this unfortunate planet of the electronic educator.'

'Did we follow in another ship?'

'Yes, as soon as we realised where the escaping ship was heading – but it was two hundred Earth years before we landed here.'

'And finally, when we arrived, I was deposited on the

84

Browns' doorstep, no doubt to mingle with other children and remain inconspicuous.'

'You have calculated the truth well,' Guardian Angel said admiringly. 'I'm afraid we had to erase your memory to help you fit into Earth ways more easily.'

'Which is why I still can't remember anything before I was seven years old?'

'Exactly – but we can reinstate your memory at any time.'

Hudson wasn't sure he wanted to remember. A part of him yearned to know about his brief childhood on Alcatron . . . though it couldn't have been very happy.

'What about the "Joe"? Why is he called Mokee *Joe*?'

'So many questions,' GA sighed.

Hudson sensed the reluctance to answer this question. He repeated it.

For the first time, GA's steadfast voice began to quiver.

'Your mother's name was Joetan-3-ergon, or Joe, as your father referred to her.'

Hudson went very quiet. He couldn't quite take it in. 'You mean he named the terminator after my mother?'

'I'm afraid so. It was some sort of warped dedication to her memory. Remember, your father held you responsible for her death.'

Hudson wanted to burst into tears, but he kept his mouth set tight. 'And now all my father's hatred is being carried around in Mokee Joe. No wonder the monster is determined to get rid of me. My father really was quite mad, wasn't he?'

GA tried his best to sound comforting. 'Yes, at the end – but initially he was a kind and good man and one of the cleverest and most respected scientists to inhabit our planet. Don't ever forget that.'

Feelings of pride, love, frustration and anger flowed through Hudson's mind, but finally a heavy feeling of sadness welled up inside him.

'I have to go,' Guardian Angel said suddenly. 'There is an exciting development regarding possible transport back home. I have begun to make some contact with the Earth authorities, but the situation is very sensitive. It is inevitable that the Earth people will soon begin to ask you questions. For the time being keep everything to yourself and your two friends. I will be staying close. The battle is looming again and you will need my help and all your new strength in the days ahead . . . and, of course, Molly and Ash – always keep them close . . .'

'But before you go, tell me about this transport,' Hudson said urgently, trying desperately to get his mind back to the present. But much to his dismay, the familiar figure of his uncle faded and disappeared.

He looked back to his pillow and still his other self slept on. Perhaps if he just lay down, he would re-enter his physical body and wake up properly. Or maybe he would sleep on peacefully until morning. And just as he was thinking about the possible outcomes, the door of his bedroom opened and Mrs Brown walked in.

'Hi, Mum,' Hudson said instinctively. But of course, she heard nothing.

Hudson watched as she smiled down at his sleeping face and stroked his hair gently.

'Oh, Hudson,' she said quietly. 'I do love you. Whoever you are, wherever you come from, you'll always be special to us.'

Hudson watched as tears formed in her eyes.

'I know you'll leave us one day. Don't ask me how I

know – it's a mother's instinct, I suppose.' She leaned down and kissed Hudson's cheek and brushed away her tears before getting up to leave.

'God bless you, Hudson,' she whispered as she closed the bedroom door again.

Hudson lay back down. His mind was swimming with all that GA and Mrs Brown had said and he put his hand to his face. He wasn't sure whether he was asleep or awake right now, or which part of him was real or unreal. *But one thing was for certain – the tears running down his cheeks most definitely felt wet.*

Tuesday – two days before the Scrubs Lower School Run. A dour mood was beginning to fall over the lower half of the school. Small groups of Years 7, 8 and 9 stood huddled in the playground, muttering and grumbling to each other. A thick, grey drizzle fell over everything and compounded the dreary atmosphere.

Ash tried to create a bit of warmth and rubbed his hands together. 'Are you sure it wasn't another one of your nightmares, Hudson?'

'I think Hudson has learnt to tell the difference by now,' Molly answered in a reprimanding tone of voice.

Hudson wasn't quite so sure. 'It was the most weird experience . . . can you imagine all this going on in my bedroom – at midnight?'

Ash pointed out that he couldn't imagine such a thing happening to him and that if it had, he would have screamed out of the house and run off down the street.

'That figures,' Molly said sharply. 'Run first and ask questions later. Typical!'

Ash looked at Molly and frowned. 'Hey! Why are you such a grumps this morning? Did you have a bad night as well?'

'Sorry!' Molly apologised. 'I'm thinking about Thursday. You know how much I love running.'

'Like loads of other people around here,' Hudson added.

They scanned around the surrounding long faces and just as the drizzle turned into solid, heavier drops of rain, Ash's mobile sent out two shrill beeps.

'Somebody's texting me,' Ash said, to nobody in particular. He took his mobile from his pocket and tapped on the buttons.

Hudson watched with interest as Ash read the message to himself. 'Come on – don't keep us in suspense! Who is it?'

'That's just it – they don't say,' Ash answered, sounding just as intrigued as Hudson. 'It just says that you're to meet at the old hideout – tonight – at seven.'

The school bell sounded and the trio walked towards the school building, thankful to be heading out of the rain.

'Thirteen, Kiln Street – up by the old brickworks?' Ash added, placing the mobile back in his inside pocket.

'Guardian Angel?' Molly asked, flicking the rain from her ponytail as she walked into the warmth.

'It must be,' Hudson replied thoughtfully. 'Are you two up for it?'

Molly was already hanging up her coat. '*I* am,' she replied without hesitation.

'Sorry, guys,' Ash said with a guilty look on his face. 'It's IT club on Tuesdays and I can't afford to miss it – I'm halfway through a training module.'

'That figures!' Molly muttered, brushing her hair and looking straight at Hudson. 'Leave him! It's not a problem. We'll be fine. And you never know when Ash's computing skills might come in useful.'

Molly smiled at him and Hudson read her thoughts. She was thinking that she and Hudson really needed all the help they could get – the situation was becoming very frightening, but she would always be there by his side.

Hudson smiled back at her, took his coat off and hung it on the peg next to hers and then they went off to lessons.

Hudson walked with his familiar big strides. 'Ten to seven – we'll just make it,' he said, staring straight up the towpath.

Molly nodded in agreement. They walked on past the old brickworks. 'Remember when I gave that big creep the trip of a lifetime?' she said, half laughing, but with a definite trace of nervousness in her voice.

'Oh my God . . . the shock on his scary face. Molly, you were brilliant that day.'

Molly smiled to herself and walked on with bigger strides than Hudson, and then he took bigger strides still, so that it became a game and a few seconds later they were both sprinting up the towpath until they arrived at the junction of Kiln Street.

Molly was the first to turn off the towpath into the

cobbled street. Hudson walked by her side and they both put their hands in their pockets and surveyed the scene.

Hudson remembered the squalor of a year ago. Now it was even worse!

Great tussocks of yellow grass and weeds sprouted from the cobbles, stretching out in front of them. The whole street was strewn with all manner of man-made rubbish, including several abandoned, burnt-out cars and the wreckage of an old lorry with all of its wheels missing.

Molly linked arms with Hudson and they walked down the middle of the road surveying the crumbling terraced houses on either side.

'Hudson – have you noticed anything?' Molly asked, squeezing his arm even tighter.

'Yes – all the houses are boarded up. Even the one where the nosy old woman lived.'

'Exactly. I think everybody's gone. The street's completely deserted.'

Many of the old streetlamps were broken, adding to the gloom, and Hudson began to feel anxious. They stopped outside number 13 and looked in disbelief at the state of the house. Every window was boarded up and the door, with 'weirdo' still daubed on it, was almost hanging off; several stout planks of old floorboarding had been hammered across the rotting doorframe.

'Hudson, do you really think that Guardian Angel would be back in there?'

'That's what's bothering me. I'm not so sure now – not after being hounded by the neighbours and eventually arrested by the police. It must have been so humiliating.'

Hudson peered between the boards into one of the

downstairs windows, but the grime was so thick and everything so dark . . .

'It's no good, Molly. I can't make anything out.'

Molly looked nervously around, but there wasn't a sign of life anywhere. And all the time it was getting darker – a strange and sinister atmosphere crept along the old cobbled road.

Hudson took a torch from his pocket and shone it between the boards hammered across the door. 'And there's something else I'm not happy about,' he whispered to Molly – though he wasn't quite sure why he was whispering. 'Guardian Angel would have said something last night, in my bedroom, surely. He would have told me he was back here again. But he never mentioned it.'

'Perhaps he forgot,' Molly suggested, a slight tremor sounding in her voice. 'Why don't you concentrate now and try to contact him – it's got to be worth a go.'

Poking his head between the boards barring the doorframe, Hudson craned his neck, straining to see through. His torch beam lit up a depressing scene: rotting floorboards, carpets long since gone, peeling, flowery wallpaper still lining the crumbling walls. He saw holes in the ceiling, and the hallway and the narrow stairs were clothed in ghostly shadows, leading up to a landing so dark that even his torch beam couldn't penetrate.

He leaned further forward and totally forgot about his new strength. A splintering crack resounded down the street as the boards gave way and Hudson suddenly found himself sitting in the open doorway at the foot of the stairs.

Molly squeezed past the broken planking. 'Hudson, are

you OK? Did you hear what I said? Why don't you try to contact Guardian Angel?'

'Sorry, Moll! Yes, you're right – I'll give it a go.'

Whilst Hudson went into a cross-legged position, Molly took the torch and climbed the first couple of stairs, shining it up towards the landing.

'Molly, don't go any higher, those stairs are probably rotten.'

'Look – just concentrate, don't worry about me. Find out if he's in here.'

Hudson closed his eyes and focused his mind. His head began to throb with a dull ache.

Molly climbed two more stairs and leaned forward, aiming the beam towards the very top of the landing. She could see some piles of newspapers and what looked like an old suitcase, but there was something bigger, something tall, leaning against the wall. She gingerly climbed another stair.

'Molly – there's something trying to come through . . . but I can't make it out . . . it's as if something's trying to block my thoughts . . . and I'm getting one of those headaches again.'

Molly turned and shone the beam down on to Hudson's head. 'GA's not here, is he?'

He concentrated even harder. And then he turned and looked up at her, standing there, waiting for his reply.

His eyes opened wide with terror as he focused on the nightmare moving down towards her and he opened his mouth to scream, but his voice seemed frozen and nothing would come out. He watched Molly's expression change to puzzlement. And then the scream came.

'IT'S ALL A TRAP! RUN! HE'S RIGHT BEHIND YOU – MOKEE JOE!'

Molly instinctively swung round and shone the beam back up the stairs. But it was too late – her blood froze as the seven-foot demon launched himself downwards, long clasping fingers outstretched and crackling with a sickly frying sound as they clawed towards her head.

She screamed.

Hudson could only watch in horror as his friend braced herself for the attack.

But Molly's survival instincts suddenly took over. She threw herself backwards and kicked both feet up in the air towards the monster. With gritted teeth she managed to lock her knees and thrust the soles of her feet firmly into Mokee Joe's belly region. A blinding blue flash ensued, but the rubber soles of her trainers protected her from the surge of electricity. Though caught off balance, Mokee Joe was incredibly heavy and Molly screamed with pain as her knees buckled under his weight and the sharp edge of the stairs dug into her back.

Hudson watched in utter disbelief as the monster continued forwards under its own momentum and suddenly found itself being propelled over Molly's head, her feet acting like a launching platform and sending it on its way like a guided missile down towards the doorway.

With an almighty THWACK Mokee Joe's head struck the one remaining plank still attached to the doorframe. A high-pitched electronic squeal followed as a rusty six-inch nail sticking out from the rotting wood penetrated deep into the monster's scalp.

'Wow! How did you do that?' Hudson shrieked, leaping to his feet and rushing to help her up.

Molly, badly shaken, rubbed her back and winced with pain. 'Hudson, just get us out of here!'

Mokee Joe rolled out into the street and struggled to his feet. Hudson and Molly followed and watched in horror as the creature danced around trying desperately to remove the length of old floorboard still anchored to its skull.

Molly yelled at the top of her voice, 'HUDSON – LET'S GET OUT OF HERE!'

Mokee Joe, complete with wood still hanging from his head, made a strange howling sound and moved towards them – the familiar blue glow beginning to emanate from his body.

'Now it's my turn,' Hudson said to himself. 'Let's put this new strength to the test.'

Before Molly could say anything, Hudson walked towards his advancing enemy and took hold of the trailing plank.

She stood and watched in disbelief, rubbing the base of her spine. 'Hudson, what . . .'

But she never got a chance to ask what he was up to.

Hudson began turning in a circle, pulling with enormous strength on the piece of wood still attached to his enemy's head.

Round and round he went, anchoring his heels into the cobbles. Meanwhile, Mokee Joe, head down and his body crackling with blue bolts of electricity, had no choice but to go round in faster and faster circles with him.

As the electric blue glowed brighter, Hudson swung faster. He knew there was no way the surging current could pass through the plank of wood into his own body. He wasn't good at science for nothing!

But just when Hudson thought he'd well and truly got the upper hand, things took a turn for the worse. His enemy had new strength as well and Hudson suddenly sensed the Mokee Man's muscle power being transmitted into the plank. The point quickly arrived where it was difficult to tell who was spinning whom. Mokee Joe was taking control of the situation.

Now the two figures were spinning even faster and to his horror Hudson realised that his enemy was in control. His head began to whirl. He was losing it and panic filled his brain. He had no choice but to let go . . . and as he did so his momentum sent him reeling down the road so that he landed in a crumpled heap.

Looking up, his vision veiled in dizziness, he could just make out Mokee Joe finally pulling his head free from the plank and moving towards him. Molly screamed at him to get up.

'QUICK, HUDSON – RUN FOR IT!'

But it was too late. The monster towered over him, glowering with a demonic, smug expression. A stale, oily smell surrounded his gangly frame.

Hudson tried to wriggle away, but knew it was hopeless. He struggled in vain as Mokee Joe lifted him like a baby into the air and held him aloft in outstretched arms, like some sort of offering to the gods.

Molly yelled in frustration and put her hands to her eyes as Mokee Joe threw Hudson a full twenty metres so that his body struck the windscreen of an old abandoned Morris Minor. A cracking, ringing sound followed, echoing up and down the street as a million shimmering glass fragments rained on to the cobbles like jewelled hailstones.

Molly screamed in frustration as Hudson finished up in a tangle on the back seat of the old car, rusty upholstery springs sticking into every part of his body. She ran over, wrenched the back door open and managed to pull his battered body free from the car and on to the cobbled road.

As she knelt over him, cradling his head in her arms, they could only watch in helpless horror as Mokee Joe moved in for the kill.

Hudson stared up at Molly's face, sure that this would be the last time he would look into those big, brown eyes – wide with terror at this particular moment. And just as he thought all was lost, that he and Molly would be wiped out together, an oh-so-familiar voice sounded clearly in his befuddled brain.

'You must be much more wary in future. I warned you that your enemy is stronger and learning new tricks with every passing hour. You may not be so lucky next time. Have Molly drag you into the shadows and say nothing – but learn from this encounter.'

As Mokee Joe moved ever closer, Hudson realised just how dazed and confused he was. How could he possibly be lucky? His time was up. He was about to be finished off – worse than that – Molly was too. GA must have finally flipped . . .

But then Molly tensed and he sensed that something other than Mokee Joe was happening.

'Hudson! I don't believe it – there's a flashing blue light at the end of the road. There's a police car heading towards us.'

They watched and waited, held their breath as Mokee Joe looked at them with hate-filled eyes, lying there helpless amongst the cobbles, and then looked back towards the slowly approaching police car.

Hudson was sure Mokee Joe would finish him off. It was his sole purpose for being here, wasn't it? Nothing else really mattered.

But he was wrong – the monster reacted to the police presence by dashing straight back into the derelict house and disappearing into the shadows.

Hudson heaved a massive sigh of relief and somehow managed to stagger to his feet. 'Quick! Molly – hide! We've got to get out of here without involving the police.'

'But, Hudson, you're hurt.'

'I'll be fine – a few bruises, that's all. Come on – let's go!'

As he and Molly slipped quietly down an alleyway and back to the towpath, Hudson suddenly realised that without his new strength he would almost certainly have been dead. No normal human being could possibly have survived that throw through the car windscreen. He knew it and Molly knew it.

Hudson put his arm around Molly and they helped each other back towards the relative safety of 13, Tennyson Road.

As she limped by his side and held her back, still wincing with pain, he wanted to hug her and hold her tight. Yet again she'd got the better of Mokee Joe. She was almost proving as much of a menace to his enemy as he was.

As they crept along, the familiar voice sounded again in Hudson's head.

'*Are you OK? I tried to warn you as you entered the old house, but the creature's thought waves are getting* stronger. *He projected a mental barrier around your subconscious and closed me out.'*

Hudson stared ahead, concentrated and reassured Guardian Angel that he was OK. He admitted that it was his fault and he should have been more careful. He would have to learn to be one step ahead of his enemy and not the other way round.

'The police car?' Hudson asked nervously. 'Was it a coincidence it turning up like that?'

'*There is no such thing as "coincidence",'* GA replied. '*This is an Earthly term. Every event that occurs is according to the Principle of Universal Circumstance. One day you will understand, but it will be many Earth years before the people on this planet work it out.'*

Hudson remained quiet and GA sensed his inability to understand.

'*Let's just say for now,'* GA continued, '*that I was able to plant the suggestion into the mind of the policeman that he ought to check out the deserted street.'*

'So it was you after all that saved—' Hudson started.

'*Enough,'* GA interrupted firmly. '*You must get yourself and your friend home safely. You should be quite secure in your home domain. It is unlikely that Mokee Joe will strike in a place where he has already attracted such attention. Remember, he learns from experience – and so must you!'*

'So maybe Candleshed will always be safe in future?' Hudson suddenly thought to himself. 'He certainly attracted attention there.' But this time there was no reply. His Guardian Uncle had gone.

Molly tugged at his sleeve. 'Are you OK, Hudson? You've gone very quiet. Are you communicating with GA?'

'Yes, sorry! But don't worry – I think we're quite safe. Let's get home.'

They turned into Tennyson Road and the streetlamps shone out a welcome – even more so after GA's reassuring words about MJ rarely striking in the same place twice.

Hudson thought to himself, 'If only I could meet up with GA again; there's so much I'd like to know and so much he'd probably want to tell me . . .'

But his thoughts were interrupted as Pugwash jumped down from off the gate of number 13 and ran down the street to greet him.

That night, after walking Molly home, Hudson took a long, soothing soak in his beloved soap bubbles. He was so racked with pain that he could hardly undress himself. But after his bath and pulling on his pyjamas, he was surprised to find that all his battle pains had completely disappeared. What's more, the following morning, he could hardly believe that there wasn't a single bruise or scar on his entire body.

Happy in the knowledge that his new strength was still climbing to incredible levels, Hudson set off for school feeling slightly reassured. And then he remembered that Thursday was now only one day away, the day of the school run, and all good feelings immediately evaporated. Every instinct he had was telling him that in some way this event was going to lead to disaster – how and why he didn't know, *but disaster was definitely on the cards.*

11

See HOW
They RuN

Hudson looked around the classroom. He looked out of the window and across the empty playground towards the railings. He looked back across the crowded classroom and through the door into the corridor. He leaned down to his schoolbag and looked inside.

'He definitely won't be hiding in there,' Molly teased.

Hudson grunted and glanced out of the window again. Molly knew that his head was full of Mokee Joe and his possible whereabouts. It was getting to the stage where he half expected his enemy to appear from anywhere – and at any moment. It was getting on his nerves and the girl sitting by his side knew it. But right now Molly only had eyes for the queue of pupils snaking around the edge of the classroom, leading up to Mrs Russell's desk.

'Look at them all with their sick notes and excuses,' Molly whispered to Hudson. 'There's nobody hates school runs more than me, but you wouldn't catch me queuing amongst that lot . . . I can't be doing with all this skiving out of things when you're perfectly healthy!'

Hudson nodded. Molly had her arms folded tightly across her chest – a sure sign she was annoyed. She'd already been excused from having to do the run because of her injured back – her mum had telephoned first thing – but Hudson had no doubt that she would have just got on with it if she'd had the chance.

They both looked at Bertie Small as he burst into tears.

'It's no good crying,' Mrs Russell was saying to him. 'The next time you write a perfect excuse note just make sure that you don't sign it with *your own name*. Now go and sit down!'

Hudson and Molly giggled as Mrs Russell frowned and put the forged excuse note in the waste bin.

The next forged note also failed. It seemed that this was well written too, like Bertie Small's, but Mrs Russell was no fool. The note explained that Emma Downton had badly sprained her right leg, but when Mrs Russell accepted the note, she noticed that Emma limped away on her *left* leg. 'Nice try, Emma – but you'd better learn to distinguish between left and right if you're to be a good trickster. NEXT!'

Several other forgeries failed owing to a considerable number of spelling errors and then Mrs Russell got angry and shouted so loudly that most of the others still in the queue decided to abandon their attempts and sit down quietly.

And finally it was Karen Blott's turn.

Karen smiled sweetly whilst the teacher read her note.

'OK, Karen. I'm sorry you've got an ingrown toenail and you're having an operation next week. You'd better be careful and stay in this afternoon – can you find some work to do? I don't want you doing nothing.'

Hudson and Molly gave each other a knowing look.

Karen looked around at the rest of the class and gloated. And then she smiled sweetly down at Mrs Russell. 'Of course I'll find something to do, miss. It'll be a good opportunity for me to catch up on some Maths.'

'Good girl, Karen – off you go. I'll just hand this on to Mr Fotheringill. Now, are there any more notes? No . . . ? Thank goodness for that!'

Mrs Russell got up to leave. 'OK, get your books ready for morning lessons – I'll be back in a minute.'

Karen smiled innocently and as soon as the teacher disappeared from the room, she almost leapt out of her seat and raised her arms in triumph.

'YEESSSS! And I wrote it all on my own, without any help, no spelling mistakes . . . And a good forged signature! Not my own signature like you, you dork, Bertie Small.'

'So you wrote it all by yourself, did you, Karen?' said Mrs Russell walking straight back into the classroom with an air of triumph. 'Well done. Now you can do the run this afternoon and I'll be arranging for you to tidy up the girls' changing room afterwards. Ingrown toenail indeed! I will be contacting your parents about this. And let this be a lesson for all of you . . .'

While Mrs Russell delivered her lecture, Karen sat down and stared at the floor, all the time muttering and grumbling under her breath. Hudson and Molly sniggered uncontrollably behind their books.

And so it was that two hundred and twenty-seven pupils lined up for the Scrubs Lower School Run at two o'clock that very afternoon.

'ON YOUR MARKS . . .' Mr Fotheringill raised his flag and put on his most serious expression. A few of the pupils braced themselves and looked keen; a good few others looked worried – anxious to get the ordeal over with; but most just shrugged their shoulders in depressed acceptance and muttered to each other.

'GO!'

Hudson watched with interest as Scott Masters sped away. He tore off like a bullet with a grim expression of determination written all over his square features. A few other keen types went after him, but most sauntered off at snail's pace. Hudson set off somewhere around the middle of the field and jogged at a comfortable pace, his intention to observe and keep a lookout for anything untoward. Ash was by his side and Karen Blott nearby, along with a couple of her friends.

Molly had volunteered to act as a marshal and accompany Mrs Russell in standing alongside the course and cheering everyone on their way. On Hudson's advice, she'd managed to persuade the teacher to stand near to the biscuit factory, near to the hole that still remained in the wire fence – Hudson and Ash referred to it as the 'Mokee Hole'.

'COME ON . . . GET A MOVE ON . . . YOU CAN DO BETTER, SMALL!' Mr Fotheringill yelled at the top of his voice, taking up a position at the rear and only needing to walk with slightly bigger strides to keep up with Bertie Small.

'Hudson – do you really think Mokee Joe will appear with so many people around?' Ash asked, jogging by his side. Hudson tried to look over the sea of heads to the front of the pack. 'I wouldn't put it past him. Remember, when you say *people* you really mean *kids* – and that's what brings him out. It's what makes him happy – striking at *kids*! We need to have all our senses on full alert – keep looking and listening.'

A cold drizzle started falling on to the cracked pavements of Danvers Green. Within five minutes Scott Masters had opened up a lead of about two hundred metres. He was out on his own – streets ahead, literally.

'Well done, Scott!' Molly shouted, pleased that someone had actually got to where she and Mrs Russell were standing.

Mrs Russell jerked her umbrella up and down enthusiastically. 'Yes – keep it going!'

Scott gave them a quick glance – a slight smile – and accelerated away with a proud look on his face.

And then, out of nowhere, he appeared – Mokee Joe – in all his horror.

'Oh my God, he's here!' Molly shrieked as Mrs Russell watched in disbelief.

'*He's here!*' The voice of Guardian Angel sounded in Hudson's head.

'He's here!' Hudson whispered urgently to Ash. 'He's struck – somewhere up ahead.'

Meanwhile, Scott Masters was completely unaware of anything – until he heard Molly's scream.

'SCOTT! WATCH OUT – YOU'RE BEING CHASED!'

For the first time, the young athlete looked back and

saw the tall, shabby figure hurtling up behind him. It unnerved him, but it would be a simple matter of changing up a gear and leaving the strange guy behind.

And so Scott put on a spurt and almost chuckled to himself.

Molly's screams sounded further away now. 'SCOTT! HE'S GAINING ON YOU!'

Again, he looked behind and saw to his horror that the gangly figure had made up a lot of ground. Now it looked more threatening – running with a stooping, scurrying sort of movement, like a fast-moving spider.

He decided to pull away at full sprint – the famous Scott Masters scorching sprint – in top gear . . .

And so after another ten seconds, breathing heavily, Scott turned again – confident this time that his strange pursuer would be left well and truly behind – *and his blood froze*. He couldn't believe his eyes. The chaser was even nearer now.

For the first time he could see the long clasping hands reaching out, shooting out some type of crackling electricity – like forked blue lightning – and the face drawing nearer, horrible in its detail.

And just when Scott Masters thought he couldn't possibly go any faster, that it wouldn't be humanly possible for a thirteen-year-old to gain any more speed, Mokee Joe accelerated and came within metres of him, bringing his horrific features into full view.

Scott looked back at that alien face with its demonic, sneering, hideous expression, and suddenly found he was able to change up to a previously unknown gear, and run at a speed he wouldn't have dreamed possible. As adrenaline pumped through his veins he felt his trainers growing hot under the soles of his feet, his lungs gasping to bursting point as he desperately tried to escape the bony clutches of the devil creature.

He dared not look behind any more and tried desperately to keep up the blistering pace.

Guardian Angel relayed to Hudson everything that was happening, but neither of them was able to do anything to help.

Scott kept up his superhuman pace for two minutes and thirty-three seconds before having to slow to a mere sprint. The sound of heavy footsteps directly behind him filled him with terror. Finally, he conceded defeat and looked back, expecting the worst.

But there was no one there. Much to his relief his demonic pursuer had disappeared – as if it had all been a terrible nightmare.

Meanwhile, Mrs Russell was busy phoning the police on her mobile and trying to stop the race by waving her arms at the same time. But it was too late – the main pack of runners had already arrived and was filtering past at a steady rate. Despite being occupied in looking for her two friends, Molly managed to stop some of the competitors.

'Hudson!' Molly spotted him amongst the crowd. 'He's up ahead – chasing Scott Masters.'

Hudson jogged over. 'I know. I got a message from GA.'

'Do you two know what's going on?' Mrs Russell asked, turning off her mobile.

Hudson put his hands on his hips; Ash jogged up and stood by his side.

'Well actually—' But Hudson didn't get the chance to say anything else.

Screams suddenly rang out from the crowd of runners and Hudson, Molly and Ash turned to see a distant familiar crumpled black hat standing out above the sea of heads.

'Hudson!' Molly screamed. 'He's back again!'

'I've phoned the police – they should be here soon,' Mrs Russell said anxiously. 'Meanwhile, I'll just have to warn him off myself.'

She began marching up the road towards the source of the disturbance. She let her brolly down and began folding it up, holding it point-first, ready to use as a weapon.

'No, miss!' Hudson yelled after her. 'Leave it to me! You've no idea what you're dealing with.'

But Mrs Russell took no notice and marched on.

'Hudson – do something!' Molly pleaded.

The screams spread throughout the crowd and pandemonium took over. Suddenly everyone was running everywhere – 'Like headless chickens,' someone nearby remarked.

Hudson saw the gangly figure of his enemy and made towards him. As he drew nearer, he saw to his horror that the evil fiend had grabbed one of the runners – a short, stocky boy called Sam Warnock – and was holding him by the neck and pressing him to the ground.

'LEAVE HIM! LET HIM GO!' Hudson screamed into the distance.

Mokee Joe was still about twenty metres away, but he was only too aware of Hudson's approach. He suddenly lifted the Warnock boy into the air and held him high above his head, just like he'd done with Hudson in Kiln Street.

Most of the runners had gone on, sprinting in sheer panic to get away from the attacker – only a few braver ones stayed back and tried to help the unfortunate victim. Karen Blott and her friends had taken up station by Mrs Russell's side, their hands over their mouths, looking on with terror-filled eyes.

'PUT HIM DOWN!' Hudson screamed, running towards Mokee Joe with clenched fists.

When Hudson was about ten metres away, Mokee Joe did just that.

He threw his victim high into the air and straight at Hudson. Sam Warnock screamed and braced himself – ready to make a crash landing.

But Hudson stopped dead in his tracks, flexed his muscles and caught him, his knees buckling before they both finally fell backwards.

The small audience gasped in amazement and cheered loudly as Hudson and the boy sorted themselves from a crumpled heap and got up, almost without injury. Mokee Joe hissed in contempt and sprinted towards the high wire fence of Macalisters Biscuit Factory.

As police sirens sounded in the distance, the monster made his escape through the 'Mokee Hole' and into the biscuit factory.

'Too late again!' Molly muttered to Ash. 'That monster is always one step ahead.'

Hudson walked to the side of the road to a hero's welcome, the badly-shaken Warnock by his side. Hudson rubbed his bottom where he'd hit the ground.

Mrs Russell met the police car and was in the process of explaining what had happened when a familiar voice suddenly echoed around the rapidly-emptying street. It boomed from the direction of two very different figures coming up from behind.

'SMALL! IF YOU DON'T GET A MOVE ON IT'LL BE DARK BEFORE WE GET BACK – NOW PLEASE PUT SOME EFFORT IN!'

Hudson, Molly and Ash looked on in amazement as Bertie Small jogged meekly past, his bottom lip trembling, tears welling up in his eyes and an extremely frustrated Mr Fotheringill walking a short distance behind.

'What's happened here?' the Games teacher shouted as he spotted Mrs Russell by the side of the police car and Hudson and his friends standing in a group. Mrs Russell went over and began explaining whilst Bertie Small limped over to Hudson and looked pleadingly at him.

'I don't suppose you could help me get back to school,' he enquired meekly. 'It's like being chased by a monster with old Fotheringill trailing behind me.'

Hudson, Molly and Ash looked at one another. If the situation hadn't been so serious, Hudson had no doubt that they would have burst into hysterical laughter.

The Scrubs Lower School Run was the topic of conversation for the rest of the day and all of the next. Some amazing statistics resulted from the race and Hudson, always interested in numbers, couldn't stop talking about them to Molly and Ash.

Despite the interference of the sinister, shabby figure, Scott Masters completed the course in record time, taking an amazing four minutes off the old school record, which had stood for eleven years.

One hundred and forty-five runners achieved their personal best times, many pupils running at a pace they hadn't previously thought possible.

Over eighty runners had gone missing and had turned up back at school after the race was over. Four girls never turned up at all and were later found by the police, hiding in a deserted alleyway. The police said they were all as white as sheets and shivering like jelly, muttering something about being chased by a skinny, creepy figure straight out of a horror film.

Bertie Small achieved a special course record – the slowest time ever for any pupil taking part in the run. Mr Fotheringill was heard to say to Mrs Russell after the race that a tortoise with one foot could have got round quicker and that in future he would sign Bertie's forged excuse note himself.

That night, whilst spreading some butter on a thick piece of toast, Hudson forgot himself and broke the knife in two, cutting one of his fingers. After Mrs Brown had dressed the cut and put on a plaster, he sneaked down the garden into Candleshed. The moon was only crescent-shaped now, but it was a clear night and the opportunity was still there to make more observations and scribble on his notepad.

Some time later, he walked back to the house. He was so deep in thought that he forgot to open the back door and walked straight into it, almost breaking it off its hinges. In a daze, he turned and went over to the old garden bench. He sat on it, gazed up at the stars and thought about his increasing strength.

Why am I getting stronger? It's something to do with me

*being from another planet, I'm sure of it. But how strong
am I going to get – strong enough to deal with Mokee Joe,
hopefully? Maybe I'm as strong as Mokee Joe already.*

But then Hudson thought back to the incident in Kiln
Street and how his enemy had got the better of him.

A loud meowing brought Hudson back to the present.
He looked up and saw Pugwash on the roof of the brick
store shed and this gave him an idea. He decided to put
his strength to the test.

He walked up to the wall of the store and stood with
palms pressed against the bricks.

I'd better not do any real damage, Hudson thought to
himself. *I just want to see if I can make any impression* . . .

He concentrated hard and pushed. Nothing happened.
He pushed harder. Still nothing happened – not even a
small crack or the slightest sound of something starting
to give.

OK – one last try . . .

Hudson closed his eyes and focused himself totally on
his task. He felt the energy surging from every muscle in
his taut body, channelling itself down his arms and into
his pressing hands. He pushed and grimaced and felt the
blood rush into his face, until it seemed his eyes were
going to burst out of their sockets.

But still nothing happened – except that Pugwash
jumped down from the roof looking extremely nervous.

Hudson reluctantly gave up and went into the house.

'Oh, it's you,' Mr Brown said, walking into the kitchen.
'Are you in or out, lad?'

'I'm in now, Dad. I'm off up to my room and then I'm
going to turn in – I'm tired out.'

'It's all that stargazing, son – I'm sure it's not good for

you. I don't suppose you saw my spade out there, did you? I think I left it out.'

'No, but I wasn't really looking. Do you want me to help you find it?'

'No – it's OK, lad. You get yourself off. I'll see you in the morning.'

Hudson went up to his room and lay fully clothed on the bed. His mind swirled with confused thoughts.

In one way he felt relieved that he'd made no impression on the brick store – the failure made him feel more normal, more like Molly and Ash. And yet in another way he hated the thought that Mokee Joe might have succeeded and pushed the wall down. As far as his enemy was concerned, Hudson knew he would always have to be at least one notch higher on the strength and cunning scales. Only then could he succeed in his purpose – to get rid of Mokee Joe for ever.

Still fully clothed, Hudson fell asleep, and for once he drifted into a deeper, less-troubled sleep.

He never heard the scraping, clanging sound as Mr Brown placed his beloved stainless-steel spade in the brick store. He never heard his adopted father slam the door shut and lock it with the big padlock. He never even heard the sinister rumbling sound as one entire wall of the brick store cracked from bottom to top followed by an almighty crash as it collapsed into a heap of dusty rubble.

Thankfully, he never heard Mr Brown's curses ringing through the crisp night air, washing over the garden and carrying away up to the moon and stars.

12

Men in Black

If the weekend passed without further incident, then the following Monday made up for it. Things got very interesting at the Scrubs during morning break.

'Who do you think those guys are?' Molly asked, staring in the direction of the school gates.

'Police – in plain clothes, and probably some sort of officials,' Hudson replied.

Ash gazed in admiration at the three jet-black Daimlers. 'Wicked number plates!'

Hudson and Molly nodded.

'GSU 1, GSU 2 and GSU 3,' Molly read out aloud. 'That must mean something.'

Hudson didn't say anything. He was too busy watching the six men, all dressed in black suits and carrying briefcases. They walked across the playground in single file towards the headteacher's office.

'Government Special Unit,' Ash stated knowingly.

Hudson looked at Ash in admiration. He was always so matter-of-fact – and yet he was so intelligent without even realising it.

'If you ask me,' Ash continued, 'they're here to follow up reports of Mokee Joe. Look at all those laptops – very impressive.'

'You're exactly right, Ash,' Hudson said, almost smiling. 'Buggles is going to get a right old grilling.'

Molly walked over, grabbed Hudson's arm and looked at him straight in the face. 'But—'

Hudson interrupted and smiled back at her. 'Yes, I know what you're going to say. They'll link Mokee Joe to us – from what happened before. It was obvious that it would only be a matter of time before someone started to ask us questions – GA warned me this would happen.'

Ash suddenly looked worried. He put his hands in his pockets and scraped the ground with the sole of his left foot. 'And then *we'll* get a right grilling!' he muttered.

Molly put a steadying hand on each of Hudson and Ash's shoulders. 'Look – we've nothing to worry about. It's not as if *we've* done anything wrong.'

'No, we don't need to worry,' Hudson agreed, grabbing his two friends by the wrists, 'but we do need to get our stories to match.'

'So do we regard them as friends or enemies, Hudson?' Ash asked, his eyes growing wider.

'Both – in a way,' Hudson replied. 'They probably think they're helping, but in some ways they're just interfering in things they don't understand.'

Molly took her wrist back and folded her arms. 'So we need to keep them out of it – not let on to what's really happening,'

Hudson thought back to GA's recent request – to keep everything quiet for the time being. 'Exactly!' he said, admiring Molly's common sense. 'Come on, we'll have a quick discussion before the bell.'

The three friends ran across the yard and stood in a huddle by the side of the school boiler house, just as the last of the smartly-dressed officials disappeared up the steps into the main entrance.

During Lesson Five Molly was called out to see the head.

As she walked out of the room, she turned and looked at Hudson. He put one thumb up to wish her luck and crossed the fingers of his other hand behind his back.

She returned about ten minutes later and to Hudson's relief had a smile on her face. She gave him the thumbs-up sign, and he waited to be called out himself – but much to his astonishment, nothing happened.

A short time later, the bell sounded for lunch and Hudson almost dragged Molly down to the dining hall to hear what she had to say.

The smell of greasy, over-cooked food filled their nostrils as they sat down to eat. Ash joined them and they each tried to chew food and splutter out words at the same time – trying to catch up on all that had happened.

It turned out that Ash had also been called out of his lesson and interviewed after Molly. Hudson couldn't understand why *he* hadn't.

'So come on, what did they say?' Hudson asked impatiently, looking first at Ash and then at Molly.

With an elbow on the table and leaning her head in her hand, she held a fork in the other and played with a small heap of mashed potato. 'Buggles just sat in one corner while one of the other guys asked the questions. He sat in Buggles's seat, at his desk . . . I don't think Buggles liked that.'

'Yes, but what did he say?'

Molly hesitated and played around some more with her fork. Hudson looked at her sly smile and realised she was teasing him. 'The other guys just sat around and clicked away on laptops. I can't imagine what they were typing.'

'Moll – stop being an idiot. Please tell me what they said.'

Ash giggled and Molly looked up from her plate and smiled.

'No need to worry, Hudson,' she said at last. 'I was probably asked exactly the same questions as Ash – which really wasn't much at all. They only asked me if the crazy man on the school run was the same one we got tangled up with at Macalisters a year ago.'

'Yeah – they asked me if it was the same man who chucked my fishing tackle in the canal,' Ash went on.

Hudson looked down at his watch and began to adjust it. 'And what did you both say?'

'What we agreed – that we didn't get a proper look, but it could have been him,' Molly said.

'Good! The last thing we want is for them to scare Mokee Joe away. We need to keep him here – I've got to face up to him.'

Ash started looking nervous and spluttered rice pudding out of his mouth as he spoke.

'What's really bothering me, Hudson—'

'. . . is that they haven't called me in. I know – I can't work that out either.'

Hudson finally put a small forkful of lukewarm lasagne in his mouth and looked over the table at Molly. She was staring out of the dining-room window and across the playground. She looked back at him and opened her mouth to speak but Hudson beat her to it. 'The cars are still there and so they still might call me in this afternoon . . .'

Molly's eyes opened wide and then she screwed them up and frowned. 'If I didn't know you better, Hudson Brown, I'd say that you're reading my mind!'

'Yeah, and mine!' Ash added indignantly.

Hudson felt himself begin to blush. He looked down at his plate and pretended to struggle with a particularly tough piece of cheese topping – and then he inadvertently bent his fork so that Molly and Ash burst out laughing.

The headteacher finally called him in at three o'clock, during the last lesson of the day. It was Science with Mr Millbank, Hudson's favourite.

He walked down the corridor with butterflies beginning to flutter in his stomach. He took deep breaths. The corridor leading to Buggles's study reeked of polish, intermingled with antiseptic. It made him feel sick.

Hudson looked at the bold lettering, HEADTEACHER, on the grained, oak door and knocked nervously.

'Enter!' a voice from the other side boomed out.

As he walked into Mr Buglass's study he was greeted by a stranger smell – a mixture of ground coffee and stale pipe tobacco.

Unlike Molly and Ash's interview, the headteacher was

sitting at his own desk. The six men in black sat on plastic chairs around the edge of the study. One empty, blue plastic chair was situated in the middle of the room, directly in front of Buggles's desk. The headteacher pointed to it.

'Sit down, Brown,' Buggles ordered sternly.

Hudson was taken aback by Buggles's sinister tone and the serious atmosphere in the room. If he'd expected the same quick informal visit as his two friends, it seemed he was mistaken.

Buggles placed his hands together on the desk in front of him and leaned his big round face forward. 'Well, young Brown – you appear to be a bit of a mystery.'

Hudson started to fidget and fiddle with his watch as he sensed the strange men around the room staring intensely at him. Three of them tapped away on the keys of their laptops, looking him up and down at the same time. One of the men appeared particularly interested in his hairstyle and stared rudely.

'I'm not sure what you mean, sir,' Hudson replied meekly.

'Oh you know exactly what I mean,' Buggles snapped back, a bead of sweat forming on his large, bulbous nose. 'Don't come the innocent with me. Ever since you arrived at Scrubwood you've caused a bit of a stir – what with huge football kicks and suchlike. Poor Mr Fotheringill is still suffering with his nerves . . .'

'How did you manage to kick that ball so hard, boy?' one of the men in black suddenly asked.

Hudson shuffled uncomfortably in his chair. 'It was pure fluke, sir. I've never managed it since – I was just as surprised as anyone else.'

Another of the men in black suddenly stopped tapping on his laptop and looked straight into Hudson's eyes. 'And I gather you helped rescue one of the boys from the clutches of the man who terrorised your school run. According to your form tutor you gathered him up with great strength. Just how strong are you, boy?'

'No stronger than anyone else as far as I know, sir,' Hudson lied. He didn't like to be untruthful, but no way was he telling these snoopers all his business.

Buggles rocked back in his chair impatiently and removed his big, gold-rimmed glasses. He spoke as he began wiping them. 'I'll be honest, Brown – I've never really taken to you, what with your strange hair and all. You *seem* different and from what I've been hearing you *are* different. And "different" means trouble in my experience.'

Hudson stared hard at Buggles's fat, round face. He recognised the same sneering expression that he'd got so used to seeing on the face of his enemy. He felt hurt at the headteacher's cruel words. Staring harder into Buggles's beady eyes he found he could read some of his thoughts and it quickly became clear that the person in front of him did not like children at all. He was not much better than Mokee Joe.

He watched more beads of sweat form on the headteacher's bulbous nose. And then Hudson realised that Buggles's expression was fast turning to one of fear – as if he realised he was being analysed.

'Don't dare stare at me like that, Brown!' Buggles suddenly shrieked at him.

'Mr Buglass,' one of the men in black said calmly, 'let me take over for a minute.'

Buggles nodded, took out a handkerchief and started wiping his brow.

Hudson looked away to the man by his side and prepared for the next question. But then he realised he already knew it. He was about to be asked how long he'd lived in Danvers Green.

'How long have you lived in Danvers Green, boy?'

'Four years, sir.'

And now he's going to ask me where I lived before that, Hudson thought to himself. It was all he could do not to answer the question before it had been asked.

'And where did you live before that?' the man asked, trying his best to sound kind and caring – failing in Hudson's opinion.

'I don't know, sir – I'm adopted.'

'Ah yes – Ernest and Mary Brown, 13, Tennyson Road.'

'Yes, sir.'

'Can you tell us anything about the strange man who appeared during the school run?'

'Not much, sir. I think he was just some street person, out to cause trouble. I didn't really get a good look at him, sir.'

'Have you been to the fair recently?'

'Last Saturday, sir.'

'And did you happen to be there during the power cut – when all the lights blacked out?'

'Yes, sir – it was quite scary.'

'Did you see anything else suspicious – like the same man who appeared on the school run? Think hard, boy.'

Hudson did the opposite. He cleared his mind of thoughts of the fairground and concentrated on the mind of the man who was questioning him instead.

He knows everything, Hudson thought to himself. *He knows Mokee Joe was there, causing havoc around the dodgems, shooting out electricity – he knows the lot!*

'Sorry . . .' Hudson finally answered. 'I didn't see anything. It was too dark.'

One of the men in black, who so far had not said a word, suddenly got up and walked over to Hudson. He took a newspaper cutting from his inside pocket and passed it to him.

'Remember this?' he said in a very serious tone.

Hudson looked at the headline:

DANVERS GREEN BOY TRAPS STALKER IN BISCUIT FACTORY

Underneath was a picture of himself with his arm around Molly.

'But, as we all know, he wasn't just a stalker, was he, son? He was much more than that.'

Hudson kept concentrating. He knew exactly which questions were coming next and it gave him a chance to prepare his answers.

'I don't know what you mean,' he replied, trying to sound as innocent as possible.

'Oh, come on, son . . . I think you and that girlfriend of yours could tell us quite a story if you wanted . . . about the flour . . . the incidents in the supermarket and up at the canal. It's all on our files.'

A reassuring voice suddenly came into Hudson's head. *'You're doing really well, Tor-3-ergon. Tell them nothing. Just keep pleading ignorant. I will deal with them in my own time.'*

Hudson felt even more confident now his Guardian Uncle was with him.

'All I know is that me and Molly have had a few run-ins with a rather tall, scruffy-looking tramp. I can't understand what all this is about.'

The man put the newspaper cutting back in his pocket and placed his hands behind his back. 'Very well, if that's the way you want to play it, we'll leave it like that for now.' He looked over to the headteacher, still wiping the sweat from his face. 'Let him go back to lessons now, Mr Buglass. We'll probably return soon to ask a few more questions – we'll let you know when.'

Buggles put his hands back on the desk in front of him and tried to look relaxed.

'OK, Brown, you're dismissed. But don't think you've heard the end of this. As I said earlier, I don't much care for your type. You can guarantee I'll be keeping a close eye on you from now on. Off you go!'

Hudson was more than pleased to leave the smell of Buggles's study behind. He walked back into the fresh air and down the corridor feeling pleased with himself. He was becoming stronger at reading thought patterns and learning fast to use it to his advantage. He'd outwitted them all – he couldn't wait to tell Molly and Ash.

And then he remembered Guardian Angel, and he concentrated for a moment, but the friendly voice had gone. He suddenly felt very isolated and alone again. But this was his battle, and sooner or later he sensed that he would have to face his enemy on his own.

So he may as well get used to it . . .

13

Another period of time passed without incident, but the lack of activity only made Hudson more nervous. It was like waiting for a bomb to go off. And then he received a mysterious e-mail:

T-3-e

Go beyond the factory and look for the ruined dwelling. Onwards towards the beechwood, pass the small water and observe a gap on the left – the sign to be ignored will take you to St Michael. I will be waiting – but take care . . . I may not be alone.

*I will look for you on the next midweek day – early
evening may be best suited.*

D-3-e (GA)

Hudson was busy looking through his telescope when
Molly and Ash arrived together at Candleshed.

'What's happened now?' Molly asked, taking off her
faded denim jacket.

Hudson turned and watched as she hung it over the
back of the old armchair. The silver star on the breast
pocket glistened in the candlelight.

'Yeah, what's new?' Ash asked nervously. 'You sounded
a bit stressed on the phone.'

'Not stressed – just excited,' Hudson replied
defensively.

He placed a printout of the e-mail on the table and
Molly and Ash leaned over and read it in the light of a
purple, scented candle.

As soon as Molly finished reading it, she sat down and
started adjusting her hair.

'Come on then, bright boy,' she said to Ash in a teasing
sort of voice. 'What's it all mean?'

Hudson looked on expectantly as Ash continued to
lean over the table and study the message.

'Hmmm . . .' Ash scratched the top of his head. 'I know
where the ruins are. There's an old estate-keeper's cottage
– or what's left of it – out past Macalisters.'

'That sounds about right,' Hudson said, going back to
his telescope. 'What about *small water*?'

'That's easy,' Ash answered, still craning forward.
'There's a small pond – we used to sail boats up there

in the summer. Mum used to take us there for picnics.'

Molly carried on adjusting her purple velvet scrunchy around her ponytail and looked over the top of Ash's head. He suddenly looked back at her. 'Come on, Molly – it's time you did a bit of work. What's *midweek day* mean?'

'Wednesday!'

Hudson adjusted the angle of his telescope and sniggered at Ash's disappointed expression.

'OK . . . good guess!' Ash said indignantly. 'But what about St Michael?'

Molly rubbed her chin and thought hard.

'You don't know, do you?' Ash giggled.

Hudson looked over at Ash . . . stared hard . . . focused on his cheery expression.

'And you don't know either,' Hudson stated firmly.

Ash swung round. 'Well, no, actually I haven't got a clue, but how . . .'

'Sorry!' Hudson said apologetically. He quickly turned back to his telescope and looked through the eyepiece. He carried on speaking whilst making further adjustments. 'You've both probably seen who it's from?'

Molly nodded. 'GA.'

'You're right.'

'But what about T-3-e and D-3-e? Is it some sort of code?' Ash asked, still peering at the e-mail. 'And why send an e-mail anyway? Why not just communicate direct?'

'I think it depends on how far away he is, and whether Mokee Joe's blocking him out and stuff like that. But the main thing is that Guardian Angel wants to meet up and I'd like you two to come with me.'

Ash sat down and went a funny pale colour. 'Hudson – you don't have to be a genius to work out what *I may not be alone* means.'

Molly took a tube of chewy sweets from her jeans pocket and began handing them out. 'It means Mokee Joe might be around,' she said, with a trace of nervousness in her voice. 'That's exactly why Hudson needs us there. So we'll both be up for it, *won't we, Ash*?'

Ash looked up at her stern expression and accepted a sweet. 'OK – I'm cool about it,' he said bravely.

But Hudson and Molly could see by the hot flustered look on Ash's face that he was far from cool.

'Look, Ash, don't worry! Trust me! Everything will work out in the end. Now come over here – and you too, Molly – there's something I want you to see.'

Hudson beckoned them over to the telescope.

'Not Orion again, Hudson,' Ash moaned at him. 'I've seen it so many times I know it off by heart.'

'No, not Orion. I want to show you the moon.'

Molly looked at him curiously, then she turned to look out of the window.

'You don't need a telescope to see the moon tonight – look, it's right there in front of us, big and bright.'

'Well, take a closer look through this,' Hudson ordered, beginning to sound just a tiny bit impatient.

Ash stooped forward and peered through the eyepiece. 'Wow . . . wicked . . . what is it?'

Molly became more interested and walked over. 'Come on, Ash, move over, I want to see what all the fuss is about.'

Ash stepped back and Molly took her turn. 'Oh my God! What is it? It looks like a bloodstain.'

Ash and Molly sat down in stunned silence whilst Hudson took another look. He finely tuned the focus so that the glowing red spot became even clearer. It seemed to pulsate slightly, glowing like a burning ember. Hudson had calculated it to be about the size of four football pitches – it had grown considerably since it first appeared just over a week ago.

'Before you ask, I've absolutely no idea what it is. But I'll tell you one thing . . .'

Molly and Ash turned to face him. Neither said anything – they just waited with anxious expressions for what was coming next.

'. . . I know it's got something to do with me – and with GA and Mokee Joe. That red spot on the moon is there for a reason and it won't be long before we all find out – believe me.'

It was Wednesday, the 'midweek day', and Hallowe'en was approaching fast.

Nobody at the Scrubs in Years 7, 8 and 9 could talk about anything else but the school disco.

During morning break, girls stood in little huddles discussing what they were planning to wear, and how they were going to do their hair, whilst the boys strutted around deciding which creepy outfits, masks and ghoulish make-up to put on.

The girls were desperate to impress the boys, whilst it seemed that the boys' main interest was to frighten the life out of everybody.

Ash had already decided that he was going to go as an undertaker – provided he survived Hudson's mysterious adventure planned for that night.

Karen Blott had made it quite clear to everyone that she was going as Morticia from the Addams Family and woe betide any other girl who copied her!

Molly was going in something really special but refused point blank to tell anyone what it was. They would just have to wait until a week on Saturday.

As for Hudson – he was too busy worrying about a million other things to be interested in a Hallowe'en Disco. But to keep everyone happy he finally agreed to go as a mad professor. More than one of the other pupils thought this was entirely appropriate and someone was even overheard to say that he wouldn't need to bother too much about a disguise.

'Do you think Mokee Joe will strike during the disco?' Ash asked, his breath forming a misty vapour in the cold morning air.

Hudson rubbed his hands together. 'It's possible. Think about it – when we met in Candleshed, GA said that he's likely to strike on "a special occasion".'

'But there'll be so many people around – it could put him off,' Molly added, folding her arms and tucking her hands under her armpits to keep them warm.

'It didn't put him off at the fair,' Ash suggested, a slight tremor in his voice. 'We'll be dressed up as ghouls and suchlike, and Mokee Joe could almost hide amongst us. He'd feel completely at home.'

'But he's so tall – somebody would spot him,' Molly pointed out.

'We'd all better be on our guard. Never underestimate him – if he wants to remain undercover he'll find some way of doing it. Anyway, that's still a good way off. Let's concentrate on tonight. How about meeting at my place at half-past six? It'll only take about fifteen minutes to get to the other side of Macalisters.'

Molly and Ash agreed, just as the bell went for the start of Lesson Four.

Hudson stroked Pugwash and watched as Mr Brown kicked his slippers off and put his feet in front of the fire. The cat purred contentedly.

'*Good evening. This is the six o'clock news,*' the new television set blurted out. Mr Brown reclined in his favourite armchair and stared at the screen.

'*Scientists are still baffled by the strange red spot that appeared on the moon's surface just over a week ago . . .*'

Mr Brown scratched his head. 'I'll be beggared,' he said in his usual gruff way. 'Whatever next! They'll be telling us it's made of green cheese before much longer. I've never heard the likes of it.'

'*Scientists think it could be some sort of energy field, but why it has suddenly appeared and is concentrated in one place is still a mystery. Some religious cults are suggesting it is an omen – a sign from God.*

'*And now on to a shock Premiership result – Manchester United . . .*'

Mr Brown got up and looked out of the window. Hudson watched with interest as he stared up at the moon.

'Moon's as clear as a bell, tonight – I can't see any sign of a red spot or anything like one.'

'You need a telescope, Dad,' Hudson told him. 'It's about the size of four football pitches – you can see it from down in Candleshed if you're interested.'

'Naw . . . it's all right, lad. I'm not that fussed. The only spot that I'm really interested in is black spot – I sometimes get it on my vegetables, but it's too late in the year to be worrying about that.'

Hudson chuckled to himself and Pugwash looked up at him, still purring softly.

Mr Brown closed the curtains and sat back down.

'What are you up to tonight then, young Hudson?' he said, less gruffly than usual.

'Just off out somewhere,' Hudson answered, staring at the TV screen.

'With Molly?'

'Yes.'

'And Ashley?'

'Yes.'

Hudson watched as his adoptive father reached over for his pipe. It was on the small table by the side of his chair. 'Anywhere interesting?'

'We're going up past Macalisters – looking for a place that Ash wants to find.' Hudson carried on staring at the screen, feeling a little guilty. He hated lying, but he could hardly tell him where they were *really* going – it would worry his parents sick.

Mr Brown struck a match and lit his pipe. He stared contentedly at Hudson, blowing out great clouds of smoke and speaking at the same time. 'I wouldn't have thought there was much to find up there. It's a bit wild on the edge of the old marsh.'

'Ash used to go up there with his mum for picnics, by a small pond.' Hudson began to feel better as he told the truth again.

Clouds of thick, blue smoke filled the room and

Pugwash jumped down from Hudson's knee and sulked off towards the kitchen.

'I know exactly where you mean – we used to go up there as lads and sail our boats. By God, that's going back a bit. The old church was still up and running in them days.'

'What church?' Hudson asked, almost leaping out of his chair.

Mr Brown puffed on his pipe and looked deep in thought. 'Well I'm blowed if I can remember. Mum will know – she was always a bigger churchgoer than me.'

He turned his head and shouted towards the sound of clattering crockery coming from the kitchen, 'MARY – WHAT WAS THAT CHURCH CALLED UP BY THE SIDE OF MACALISTERS?'

Mrs Brown appeared at the doorway, drying a plate. 'St Michael's. It's a lovely little church, but the foundations started to sink and they had to close it. It's right on the edge of the old marsh, you see.'

'That's right, of course – St Michael's. I do declare my memory's getting worse as I get older. Didn't they pull it down?'

But before his wife had a chance to answer, there was a loud knocking on the door. Mrs Brown returned to the kitchen and reappeared a few seconds later, still drying the same plate. 'Molly and Ash are here, Hudson. The pair of them look a bit tense. Whatever are you up to?'

'Leave them be, Mary,' Mr Brown smiled from his chair. 'They're off to do a bit of exploring. There's no harm in that. In fact I wish I were going with them – but don't stay out too late, mind. It's already getting dark.'

Hudson slipped his leather jacket on – the one with

the flames up the back – and wondered if his father would still want to go with them if he knew what might be waiting when they got there.

14

Ghouls and Graveyards

Mrs Brown's worries and concerns were still rattling through Hudson's mind as they reached the gates of Macalisters Biscuit Factory. For once, Mr Brown had been firmly on their side, allayed his wife's fears and helped them avoid any more awkward questions.

Now, as black clouds moved across the moon and a faint breeze began to chill their bones. Hudson wondered if he ought to have stayed home and continued to watch TV with Pugwash safely tucked up on his knee.

'Do you think this could still be Mokee Joe's den?' Ash asked, shining his torch towards the hole in the high, wire fence of the biscuit factory.

'Actually, I don't,' Hudson answered confidently. 'I know the Mokee Hole's still there, but that's because they just haven't bothered to repair it. In any case, he doesn't need flour any more – he's found other ways of charging himself up.'

'How?' Ash asked, his voice full of intrigue.

'It's to do with magnetism, but other than that I'm not sure. It's complicated. GA said it's something to do with tuning in to the Earth's magnetic field.'

Ash looked very thoughtful. 'But magnetism's all around us, isn't it?'

'Yes, I think it is. So he could be getting it from anywhere.'

Molly shuddered. 'I just hope he's not hiding out wherever we're heading to.'

Everyone went quiet and said nothing for the next few minutes.

'Look! There's the pond I told you about – it's still here,' Ash exclaimed. There was still just enough daylight left to see the moonlight reflecting on the surface of the water. A startled duck quacked with fright and shot off into some dying reeds.

'What was next?' Molly asked. 'In the e-mail?'

Hudson had memorised it. '. . . *Observe a gap on the left – the sign to be ignored will take you to St Michael.*' He turned away from the pond and scanned the edge of the wood. At first, all he saw was a dark line of trees – but then he thought he saw something else and walked over to investigate. As he crept forward, the leaves rustled and whispered in the strengthening evening breeze. Darkness continued to envelop everything.

'Over here,' he called to his two friends.

'What is it?' Ash crept over and shone his torch towards where Hudson was standing. There was a small gap between the trees and an old faded sign saying:

STRICTLY PRIVATE – NO ACCESS

'This is it!' Ash whispered loudly, sounding excited.

'What is?' Molly replied, feeling slightly puzzled.

'*The sign to be ignored*. This must be it.'

And then, as Ash's torch beam lit up a spooky, overgrown footpath beyond the gap, he stood back and went very quiet.

'Well come on then – what are you waiting for?' Molly muttered. 'Give me the torch.'

Ash handed it over and watched in awe as Molly ploughed through the gap and into the undergrowth. Without hesitating she headed off into the darkness, Hudson following close behind.

'Come on, Ash – stay close,' Hudson said reassuringly.

Ash, suddenly realising that he was about to be left on his own, quickly followed.

After stumbling onwards, falling over tree stumps, pushing through brambles and constantly being whipped in the face by trailing branches, Hudson was on the point of turning back. The darkness was closing in fast now and the atmosphere was getting spookier by the minute.

It was Molly who spotted the first curved stone sticking out of the undergrowth to the right of the path.

'What's that?' she asked in a whisper, pointing her torch at it.

A bank of angry clouds high above their heads moved away so that the full moon shone down, adding light to the scene in front. Now more stones were visible, some curved and others in the shape of crosses, all at varying angles to the ground.

'Uh oh . . . I know what this is,' Ash said, sounding full of dread.

And then he let out a piercing scream.

There, right in his path, a granite-grey, skull-like face glared at him from the gloom, full of menace, peering over the top of an ancient tombstone. The sight of it filled Ash with horror.

'It's a graveyard!' Molly said abruptly. 'And you're looking at a stone skull, that's all – now calm down and let's move on. The sooner we're out of here the better.'

Ash put his hand over his mouth, sighed and said nothing.

'And the next part of the message is just over there,' Hudson added, aiming his torch beyond the stones and into a clearing.

Molly and Ash looked where he was pointing and saw the dark outline of a building. They were both quick to recognise the familiar shape.

'A church . . .' they both gasped together.

'St Michael's to be more precise,' Hudson said with authority. 'I guessed as much when Dad said he could remember an old church near here – only it's not been pulled down like he thought.'

From somewhere close an owl hooted and the moon disappeared again behind a line of cloud. Everything went darker, making the outline of the old church look sharper against the night sky.

'Hudson – do you really want us to go in there?' Ash's voice quivered in the gloom. 'I don't like it . . . it looks like a perfect hiding place for Mokee Joe.'

Nobody could disagree with Ash's chilling statement.

The old familiar butterflies began to chase around as a lurching fear rose in their stomachs.

Hudson tried his best to reassure everyone. 'I'm sure GA is watching out for us. He wouldn't have asked us to come here if there was a high risk of meeting up with the Mokee Man.'

Molly nodded, bit her lip and moved to the front. She shone the torch and picked out an old paved pathway almost completely grown over with thick tufts of grass and weeds.

'Come on . . . let's get on. There's no point hanging around – let's take a look.'

They edged on further and the outline of the disused church became clearer. Now the steeple stood out black against the skyline and the silhouette of a small cross at the very top seemed to offer some sort of reassurance.

Still further, and the number of old gravestones increased, sprouting out of the ground in all directions, as if trying to bar their way. Hudson could hear Ash breathing heavily by his side.

A few more steps and a dilapidated porchway with a huge wooden door showed in Molly's torch beam. A rotting sign on the door warned:

KEEP OUT – DANGER – FALLING MASONRY

Now it was Hudson's turn to shine his torch beam on to a small window by the side of the door. Surprisingly it still contained some glass. He stopped dead in his tracks.

'I think I can see a light flickering inside. Look – through the glass . . .'

'No – I don't think so,' Ash replied, his breaths coming in short gasps. 'It's just the light from your torch reflecting back.'

'OK . . . well, let's see what happens when I switch it off.'

He clicked off the switch – the light still flickered through the window.

'There *is* somebody inside,' Molly said in a hushed voice. 'It's got to be GA.'

'I certainly hope so,' Hudson whispered in reply. 'Remember, he did say that he might not be alone! Just stay close – I'm sure we'll be fine.'

Placing his palms on the damp wood, he leaned forward and pushed on the ancient wooden door. At first nothing happened. Hudson flexed his muscles and pushed harder. This time the huge door began to move, creaking horribly on its rusted iron hinges. As it swung open, a wave of stale, damp air washed over them. They crept inside and were taken aback by the squalor and emptiness.

There were no pews or seats of any kind; in fact no furniture at all – just a vast empty space, littered with fallen masonry. They moved slowly forward, scanning the way ahead with their torch beams, their footsteps echoing on the stone floor. They saw that many of the large stone flags were gravestones, inscribed with the names of the dead occupants lying beneath their feet.

'Look!' Ash gasped in a loud whisper. 'There's somebody up at the front.'

But Hudson and Molly had already spotted the curious shape sitting on the steps leading up to where the altar had once stood. The figure held some sort of lantern and it threw out enough light for them to see that it was staring in their direction.

And then a deep voice boomed across the empty

space, resounding so loudly that Hudson and Molly almost jumped out of their skins. Ash turned to run.

'Welcome . . . I've been expecting you. Come nearer – there's nothing to fear.'

Hudson immediately recognised the voice and relaxed a little. 'OK, you guys – it's Guardian Angel.'

But Molly and Ash were still nervous. Neither of them had met their ally before and as they drew nearer and saw the strange-shaped head becoming clearer in the lamplight, their hearts began to beat faster and their instincts told them to stay back.

Guardian Angel sensed their anxiety and dimmed his lantern. 'Don't be afraid of me – I am here as a friend. Sit on the floor – here in front of me.'

The floor looked uninviting – stone slabs, cold and damp, covered in lichen and moss.

Three pairs of staring eyes watched in awe as the seated figure waved his outstretched hand and at once a warm glow seemed to radiate from the floor.

Hudson was the first to sit down. 'Wow! Incredible! It's like sitting on a hot-water bottle.'

Molly and Ash sat cross-legged by his side.

'Hey, Hudson – that's amazing. How did he do that?' Molly asked.

'Yeah, that's some trick,' Ash whispered to Hudson.

'It's all to do with simple transference of energy,' the figure in front of them said in a gentle voice. 'But to more important matters . . .'

Hudson, Molly and Ash sat and stared at the face, half-hidden in the shadows. They listened attentively as the voice spoke in a more serious tone.

'The enemy is becoming ever stronger and is able to

read or even block out my thoughts – which is why I sent you the electronic mail. The chances are that if I contact you by mental transmission he will tune in to our conversation and know our next move. For this reason the three of you need to work together closely and combine all of your human senses.'

'You mean like three sets of eyes, three sets of ears and so on?' Hudson suggested.

'Exactly!' Guardian Angel confirmed. 'And don't forget you have your ever-increasing strength.'

Ash plucked up his courage to speak to the strange figure in front. 'Why is Hudson becoming so strong? It's getting a bit weird!'

'I'm sure that you know by now that Hudson is not of this planet – he is from a faraway galaxy system where the gravitational forces are much greater than humans are used to. His increasing strength and powers are all part of his normal Alcatron development.'

Molly and Ash both looked across at Hudson at the same time. Sitting there with his strange hot-cross-bun hairstyle silhouetted against the spooky half-light and his wide shadowy eyes gazing in admiration at his Guardian Angel, the news that their best friend was actually an alien still came as a great shock. They stared at him with expressions of awe and wonder. Hudson stared back at them and read their reactions: Ash a little frightened – Molly too.

'You really are from another world . . .' Molly half told him and half asked him, her eyes bigger than he'd ever seen them before.

'Yes, it's true. But you always knew deep down that I was different,' Hudson replied.

'But we never really believed that you were *that* different!' Ash joined in. 'Hudson, this is so weird.'

Hudson felt a sense of relief. He was pleased that his two closest friends knew his secret. And he had every confidence that they would keep it. He turned back to his Guardian Uncle. 'Where is Mokee Joe hiding out? Is he still in Macalisters?'

'No – he knows it's too dangerous for him there now. He has a much better hiding place – somewhere more isolated and out of the way.'

'It wouldn't be near here, would it?' Molly asked with an edge in her voice.

'He hides amongst the extinguished life forces that surround us.'

Molly looked to Hudson again. She didn't understand.

'He means *here*,' Hudson said with some urgency. 'The tombstones outside mark the dead – or the "extinguished life forces", as GA calls them.'

'Oh hell – we've got to go back out there . . .'

'At the present time, you should be out of danger,' Guardian Angel reassured them. 'I tracked him earlier to a place far away.'

'Do you know where?' Hudson asked, filled with curiosity.

'He's hiding in a factory on an industrial estate, about ten miles away. It's a factory that makes magnets.'

Hudson gulped. 'His new energy source,' he said, turning towards his two friends. But he could see by Molly and Ash's faces that they were too shocked to take it all in.

GA continued, his voice growing ever softer, 'I brought you here tonight for a reason. I want you to remember this place and think of me. I will be here – and you may well need my help over the forthcoming days.'

Hudson began to fidget. 'In what way? Is Mokee Joe about to strike again? I think you said something about "a special occasion"?'

'You have remembered well. That is how it is. Things are fast approaching a conclusion. I have tried to read the monster's mind more than once, but always he blocks out the most crucial information. You must prepare yourself for anything that might happen. And now you must go back – your parents will be worried.'

The three friends stood up and Hudson moved towards the seated figure.

Guardian Angel read his mind and moved the lantern nearer to his face.

This was the first time that the physical Hudson had met up with his physical Guardian Angel and maybe that was the reason why the face that lit up in front of him looked different.

No longer sinister, the eyes were not pupil-less and staring white as before – this time they were large and blue and full of kindness.

Molly whispered to Hudson, 'Now I know why you call him Guardian Angel – he's got an angel's eyes; they're the loveliest eyes I've ever seen.'

Hudson nodded. He moved closer still and looked into his uncle's face. As their eyes met, he felt a warm glow flow through his body, reaching right down into his fingertips and toes. And in those few seconds he sensed the bond he longed for. He yearned to hug his Guardian Uncle close, like a long-lost child might hug its father. He wanted to stay with him, never to leave his side, go with him back to wherever they belonged.

GA leaned forward and Hudson heard a voice whispering softly in his head. 'Take care, Tor-3-ergon. May the God of all the universe stay with you.'

'And you too,' Hudson whispered back. And then, reluctantly, he turned to leave.

With more than enough to think about, the three friends left the church and retraced their steps through the old graveyard. They did not hang about, and for once, Ash led from the front. Within a very short time they had made their way back down the footpath and on past Macalisters. Hardly anyone spoke during the return journey and Hudson sensed that Molly and Ash were just as terrified as he was of the thought that Mokee Joe may have returned from the factory, fully charged, and be lying in wait for them.

But GA's prediction was correct. Nothing happened. On this occasion, the monster had been busily occupied elsewhere. Hudson found himself wondering whether any new 'victims' had fallen foul of the evil demon's deeds.

It was such a good feeling to reach the safety of number 13, Tennyson Road and an even greater comfort when Mrs Brown provided three mugs of steaming hot chocolate.

Hudson sipped his warm drink and found himself yearning to be back in the old church – back with the only person that really understood him. One day they would be together for always and maybe even return to Hudson's true home on Alcatron 3 . . . and just when Hudson was warming to these thoughts, the horrible vision of his enemy sprang up in his head again.

Hudson shuddered. He took another swig of his

chocolate and tried to think of more pleasant images, but he couldn't get Mokee Joe out of his mind – always there, always haunting him – until the final showdown.

'Are you OK, Hudson?' Molly asked, gently elbowing him in the side. 'You've gone very quiet.'

Hudson didn't hear her. He didn't even feel her nudging him. He didn't even hear the sickening crack as his favourite, stripy china mug split from top to bottom; he'd squeezed it too tightly.

The piping hot chocolate spilled on to his lap, seeped through his jeans and still Hudson stared unfeeling into space, dreaming of the final encounter.

15

Atmospheres

In the build-up to Hallowe'en, as the 'spooky season' fell into full swing, the weather began to play its part. A huge depression moved across Britain and settled with its centre over the North Midlands. The days became darker – sometimes it hardly got light at all – rain pouring incessantly from morning to night. A chilling autumn wind blew relentlessly, driving huge banks of grey clouds across leaden skies, and the sun became a forgotten thing; its sister, the moon, challenging as the leading heavenly light by making brief appearances in the dead of night.

'Hi, guys,' Mr Gladstone shouted across to Hudson and Molly.

The two friends smiled back. 'Hi, sir,' they both shouted together.

The teacher walked over the yard towards them. 'You two looking forward to the disco? Cool gear and everything at the ready?'

'Well, I've got a bit of a disguise,' Hudson replied without too much enthusiasm, 'but Molly's keeping quiet about her outfit – she won't even tell *me* what she's going to turn up in.'

Molly folded her arms and smiled coyly up at the teacher. 'That's right, sir – it's a bit of a surprise . . .' she glanced over her shoulder and saw Karen Blott standing with Sandra Hickson – they were straining to hear what she was saying, '. . . and I don't want *anyone* finding out.'

Brinnie looked over Molly's shoulder and saw the two girls trying to hear their conversation. He chuckled. 'Well, Molly – I'm sure you'll impress and we can't wait to see what you turn up in, can we, Hudson?'

Hudson looked slightly embarrassed, nodded his head and pretended to adjust his watch, which caused Brinnie to chuckle again.

'Are you entering the dance competition?'

'No, I don't think so, sir. I'm not really the dancing type.'

'Me neither,' Brinnie smiled at him. 'If you dance as well as me it's probably a good idea to stay in the shadows and remain as well-hidden as possible.'

Hudson suddenly looked thoughtful. Words like 'well-hidden' and 'shadows' made him feel distinctly uncomfortable.

With the disco just one day away, Miss Drew had allowed Year 7s to design Hallowe'en posters and hanging decorations to adorn the assembly hall.

As usual, Hudson and Molly were working together.

They were constructing a large poster that showed a fearsome witch riding on a broomstick through a night sky laced with stars and planets. Molly was working on the witch and Hudson, of course, was taken up with painting in the stars and planets.

Hudson was so absorbed by the poster that he jumped more than most when Miss Drew shrieked out from the front of the class, 'Oh my giddy aunt – what's that?'

Hudson and Molly followed her startled gaze out of the window. The Art and Design classrooms were on the first floor of the building and afforded an excellent view out across the playground.

'It can't be!' Molly gasped.

Hudson suddenly felt chilled to the bone as he saw the tall, gangly figure protruding above the red brick wall bordering the yard. The crumpled felt hat and long greasy hair were clearly visible – though the face was completely in the shadow of the grubby raincoat collar. The figure appeared to be moving along in a very strange way.

Just as happened a year ago at Danvers Green Primary, the class moved over to the window to observe the sinister spectacle.

And then, as the figure reached the end of the wall and turned into the playground, everyone, including Miss Drew, burst out laughing.

'It's Ashley Swift. He's carrying some sort of figure,' the Art teacher cried out in a very relieved tone of voice. 'It must be for the Hallowe'en decorations. And pretty effective it looks too, I might add.'

Hudson and Molly watched in amazement as Ash struggled with the tall, creepy-looking dummy across the playground.

'I can't believe Ash would be that stupid,' Molly muttered.

'To make some sort of replica of Mokee Joe,' Hudson continued. 'No – I can't believe it either. What's he thinking of?'

Molly thumped the desk and some of the other pupils looked round.

'Just wait till break – he'd better have a good explanation.'

Hudson looked at the grim expression on Molly's face and thought that Ash better had.

They found Ash in the assembly hall, by the stage. He was sitting by his huge Mokee Joe effigy, surrounded by a gang of Year 7 pupils.

'Wow! That's one hell of a Guy Fawkes,' one ginger-haired boy was saying.

'It looks a bit like the madman that caused trouble on the school run,' added a sensible-looking girl, her voice trembling slightly.

Hudson sensed that Ash was enjoying all the attention. He and Molly stood back and waited until his group of admirers had moved away before they moved in to question him.

'Where have you been and what the hell do you think you're doing?' Molly shrieked at him.

'Yeah – what's the big idea, Ash?' Hudson asked. 'Have you flipped?'

Ash smiled back at them. 'Just calm down and give me a chance to explain.'

'This had better be good,' Molly said with a grim look on her face. She folded her arms and waited for an explanation.

'Don't you think this is a good likeness?' Ash asked the two of them, gazing admiringly at the figure sitting on the edge of the stage.

Hudson looked it up and down. From a distance it had been fairly convincing – the clothes being very similar to those of his enemy. But close up, it simply bore a fairly mediocre resemblance to a Guy Fawkes – the hands merely gloves stuffed with newspaper and the face a cheap plastic skeleton mask hidden beneath the hat and collar.

'No, not really,' Hudson replied, still sounding serious. 'What are you up to?'

'Yeah . . . come on, Ash,' Molly added. 'What on Earth are you up to?'

'OK! OK! Keep your hair on! It's like this . . . I've entered myself for the best dance act competition and this here is my partner – I thought it was about time we had a laugh at that devil's expense!'

Molly's mouth was set in a grim expression, but her lips slowly spread into a smile. 'Well . . . when you put it like that!' she said, calming down.

'I've got to admit, it sounds a great idea,' Hudson chipped in.

Ash smiled at them again. 'Exactly!'

'And if Mokee Joe does turn up at the disco,' Hudson went on, winking at Molly, 'and sees this crude likeness of himself, he'll make straight for it . . .'

'And no doubt want to find out who made it,' Molly added, smiling back at Hudson.

Hudson could see by Ash's worried expression that he wasn't sure whether he was being teased or being faced with a definite possibility. His face started to go a funny white colour.

'Hmmm . . . I hadn't really thought about that side of things. But I'm glad you appreciate it. It took me ages to put this monstrosity together – I had to go up and down our street knocking on every door to collect enough newspapers to make the stuffing. Mum and Dad let me stay up and finish it last night and then I went and slept in this morning, and that's why I was late – it was nine o'clock before Mum woke me.'

Hudson laughed. 'Well it was worth it just to see the look on all our faces when you came walking up the street past the playground! You nearly gave us all a heart attack.'

They propped up the tall, gangly figure against one of the giant speakers at the side of the stage and then took a look around the rest of the hall.

Brinnie was up a pair of steps, hanging coloured bunting around the walls, and some of the pupils in his form were helping. The curtains on the stage had already been decorated with silver stars and moons and Hudson couldn't stop looking at them. Two sound decks had been placed on the stage and some of the older sixth-form pupils were trying out a few tracks so that every now and then loud pop music reverberated through the room.

All in all, the atmosphere was building up quite nicely. Everyone sensed that Brinnie's Hallowe'en Disco was going to be a great success.

That night, Hudson sipped his drink slowly and stroked Pugwash with great affection – almost as if it might be the last time.

'You're looking a bit serious tonight,' Mrs Brown said, knitting needles clicking away madly. 'Is that chocolate OK? I may have made it a bit weak.'

'It's fine, Mum. It's just that . . .' Hudson hesitated.

Mrs Brown dropped her knitting on to her lap, turned and looked him straight in the eye. 'What is it, Hudson? What's bothering you?'

He looked back at her and had a job to stop himself throwing his arms around her neck.

'I just want you and Dad to know that if ever anything happens to me, I'll always be grateful . . .' Hudson faltered for the right words.

Mrs Brown cut in and helped him out. 'I'm sure I don't know what you mean, but you've nothing to thank us for; me and Dad have only given you back in return what you've given us – love and affection.'

Hudson felt a surge of emotion as his adoptive mum's last few words hit home – *love and affection*.

Despite all his differences and the troubles he'd brought to Tennyson Road, that day he landed on the doorstep, Mr and Mrs Brown had always stood by him and treated him in the same way as any natural parents. He really didn't deserve them.

He went back to his chocolate and Mrs Brown picked up her knitting again. Both of them carried on as if nothing had happened – no one spoke – they hardly dared look at each other.

Sitting on the edge of his bed, Hudson reached over for the little block of clear resin sitting on his bedside cabinet. He stared down at the preserved carcass of his faithful spider friend and stroked it affectionately with one finger.

'From now on I'm going to keep you with me all the time, old buddy,' Hudson whispered softly. 'Whether good luck exists or, as GA says, everything happens according to the Principle of Universal Circumstance – well, I really don't care. All I know is I feel safer when you're around – dead or alive.'

And saying this, Hudson gripped the resin block tightly in the palm of his closed hand. After a few minutes, he opened his hand and almost dropped the block in surprise. The dead spider had changed colour – from the original dull grey to a bright and vibrant shade of blue. It was as if Spiffy had come back to life – ready to help him in battle again.

'Transference of energy – that's what it is,' Hudson said to himself. 'Just like when GA heated up the stone slabs in the church. I suppose I'm getting more and more like GA – who knows what I'll be able to do next?'

With these reassuring thoughts swirling round in his head, he placed Spiffy back on his bedside cabinet and changed into his pyjamas.

He climbed into bed and found himself wondering about GA again. If he was really going to develop all his Guardian Uncle's powers then one day he might be able to will himself to leave his body and visit him – just like the time when he'd travelled over the rooftops to Kiln Street. He might even be able to home in on Mokee Joe and spy on him – the thought caused a shiver to run down his spine.

I've tested my physical strength, Hudson thought to himself; *maybe it's time to test my mental powers*.

He snuggled under the duvet and closed his eyes so that everything was in total blackness. And then he concentrated on GA's face – really concentrated. But just as he was feeling totally focused, the face of his enemy appeared instead. For some reason Hudson found it easier to concentrate on the face of Mokee Joe. Perhaps it was because he knew that face so well in every hideous detail. Suddenly, the face became so clear in his mind that it seemed real and Hudson began to feel afraid. But he concentrated harder still, more and more focus – and then all at once, Hudson's room went very cold and a strange buzzing filled his ears.

He tried to snuggle further under the duvet. But the duvet had gone. Something very weird had happened. He found himself looking up at the stars through a series of overhead cables. He could smell grass, and feel the dampness under his body. He couldn't believe it – he was outside.

And then a familiar oily smell filled his nostrils and icy-cold goosebumps spread all over his body as he realised he was not alone.

16

The Scrubs Halloween Disco

It had been the strangest of Friday nights.

After projecting his mental-self right next to his enemy, Hudson had spent most of the night awake, hardly daring to go to sleep lest he should finish up in that dreadful place again. It seemed he had managed to transport his 'other self' into a field – underneath an electricity pylon, where Mokee Joe had been stretched out absorbing the energy from the electromagnetic field. But for Hudson to find himself suddenly stretched out beside him – it was just about the scariest experience he'd ever had; especially the way in which those eyes had stared back at him, full of hatred and malice.

Thankfully, after his initial panic, the vision had quickly disappeared, but the worst thing was that when Hudson had sat bolt upright in bed, the stale oily smell was still there.

For the rest of the night, Hudson had failed to get any sleep. Much of the time had been spent going over and over things in his mind – trying to work things out and predict what was going to happen next.

It was only when daylight had filtered through his bedroom curtains that he'd felt overcome by tiredness and drifted into sleep. Mrs Brown hadn't shouted him and he'd stayed in bed until lunchtime. And even then, most of Saturday afternoon had been spent just sitting around, thinking and dozing, but all the time a tinge of nervous excitement building up inside as the Scrubs Hallowe'en Disco drew nearer.

At six o'clock, Hudson decided it was finally time to get himself ready. The first thing he did was to put the little resin block containing his late friend into his trouser pocket.

At seven-thirty Hudson walked into the Scrubs wearing a white coat, a white shirt with a small chequered bow tie, and to complete his 'mad professor' disguise, a pair of thick black-rimmed spectacles.

Molly had arranged to come later at about eight o'clock – she wanted to surprise him – and so Hudson felt strangely alone as he walked into the dimly-lit assembly hall. Nevertheless, it was a truly awesome sight that greeted him and he was almost overcome by the spectacle – Brinnie and his team had done a fantastic job.

The room was shrouded in shadows, but an array of coloured, flashing lights and special effects cut across the darkness. Hudson was spellbound by them – especially the large silver sphere that hung over the centre of the stage. A beam of light, constantly changing colour, illuminated the orb, and as it rotated slowly it reflected light patterns in all directions.

Other light sources, lasers and spots, threw a myriad of colour out across the room and all in time to the pulse of throbbing music emitting from large speakers in each corner.

The walls were decorated with large portraits of ghouls, ghosts, demons and skeletons, their faces grinning with horrible expressions in the flickering light.

The gangly figure of the mock Mokee Joe still sat to one side of the stage, leaning against one of the giant speakers. Two sixth-formers in vampire costumes stood just behind, playing music on a large sound deck. Other pupils stood around in small groups, chuckling at each other's spooky outfits – skeletons, devils complete with horns and forked tails, mummies wrapped in bandages . . . *Suddenly, Hudson sensed he was being stared at.*

He looked around just as the music changed to a haunting rhythmic beat. He began to feel excited and uneasy at the same time.

And then he saw the tall figure, standing quite still and staring straight at him.

He had no idea who or what it was.

Just a bit taller than himself, dark and mysterious under the subdued lighting, the haunting spectre was dressed in long, black, wispy material – Hudson was completely mesmerised.

It started walking towards him, almost in slow motion, moving in time to the hypnotic beat still filling his ears.

Long, shoulder-length hair, as black as the night sky,

slim curvy figure, sleek and graceful in its movement. And then the face came into view.

Hudson didn't recognise the striking eyes lined with black mascara, the long eyelashes and the lips glistening with a vivid purple hue. The face captivated him, held him in its stare without smiling, hypnotised him in the same way that Molly's eyes . . . He suddenly felt very guilty and turned his gaze away to the front of the hall. And then the figure spoke in a familiar voice.

'Hi, Hudson! Do you fancy a Coke? I'm just going over to the bar.'

Hudson looked back at Karen Blott in complete surprise. 'Oh, Karen – I didn't recognise you – you look so . . .'

'Stunning?'

'Y-yes. S-so . . .'

'Gothic?'

Hudson continued to stammer, 'Y-you l-look amazing.' He watched as Karen's face broke into a broad smile.

She grabbed hold of his arm. 'Come on, you mad little professor you – put that case down and you can buy me a drink.'

And so it was that Hudson Brown and Karen Blott went off arm in arm to the bar at the back of the hall. A fairly scary Egyptian mummy was serving them their drinks when Ash walked in, dressed as an undertaker. Hudson smiled at Karen and passed her a glass of Coke. He looked up and saw Ash walking towards them. His friend looked anxious.

Ash pulled Hudson aside. 'Molly will be here any time – come on . . .'

Hudson looked at his watch. It was two minutes to

eight. Ash was right – Molly would be here about now and he wanted to find her. As far as Hudson was concerned, the sooner the three of them were together, the better.

'Karen – I'll catch up with you later – I just need to talk to Ash for a minute.'

She shrugged her shoulders and sucked through her straw without replying. Her face said it all.

Ash grabbed Hudson's arm and they moved towards the stage. Hudson looked around. Crowds of pupils were arriving and spreading across the dance floor.

Hudson told Ash briefly about his scary night-time experience and this set the two of them thinking about Mokee Joe – would the Hallowe'en Disco be the 'special occasion' that would tempt his enemy to make a strike?

Hudson found himself wondering whether the creature would really have the nerve to make an entrance and sneak in. It would be much easier when there were lots of people around – plenty to hide amongst. The thought made Hudson feel very uncomfortable.

The music stopped and the hall continued to fill up rapidly as Brinnie appeared on the stage. 'Hi, everyone. It's good to see so many of you here. We've got a great night ahead of us and we really must get this show on the road. I'd like to start by announcing the first act in our dance competition. There are a total of six acts throughout the evening and the best will win a pair of tickets for a trip on the London Eye, so they can take their coolest date . . . and don't forget, girls – I'm always available.'

Some of the girls in the audience giggled . . .

'Anyway, move closer – especially all you guys – 'cos

here comes our first act, and you can take it from me it's going to be a hard act to follow . . .'

'Where's Molly?' Hudson whispered to Ash. 'She wouldn't have wanted to miss this.'

'I don't know,' Ash answered, looking round. 'Maybe she'll be here in a minute.'

As the crowd pushed forward, a loud blast of energetic music hit everyone's ears. Karen Blott almost climbed over the person in front to get a closer look.

And then Hudson's mouth dropped open as Molly danced out on to the stage.

The mad professor completely forgot his strength and almost flattened the three rows in front as he pushed to get closer. And then he was standing by the stage, looking up at Molly as she danced in an electrifying way to the catchy, punchy sound of a familiar hip-hop tune.

His eyes bulged in disbelief at her stunning outfit – a deep crimson crop-top decorated in silver stars and striking velvet flares in matching magenta, these too decorated below the knee with silver sequins and rhinestones.

As her body moved in perfect rhythm to the powerful beat, Hudson looked up at her face and marvelled at the gold, crescent moons dangling from each of her ears. Her hair was spiked up into two bunches, and covered in glitter.

She danced an amazing choreographed routine and he glowed with pride as she still took the time to smile down at him.

And then finally Hudson noted that in between the top of her flares and her crop-top she was wearing a glistening jewelled stud in her belly button.

His mind swirled with confused feelings and different emotions as the coloured lights flashed like lightning, reflecting from the glittering silver orb above the stage. Molly entranced him, her vision a perfect contrast to the Mokee Joe effigy still seated at the edge of the stage. As her dance continued, the audience went wild and clapped to the beat – nobody clapping as loud as Hudson and Ash.

As soon as Molly had finished her number, the Hallowe'en crowd applauded so loudly that Ash put his hands over his ears. Hudson couldn't help himself and rushed on to the stage to congratulate her. Brinnie walked on and tried to hush the crowd. He put his arms in the air and gestured to the audience. 'OK . . . OK . . . I told you it would be good.'

A few minutes later, Hudson was back at the drinks bar, but this time sipping a Coke with Molly, and staring at her in admiration.

'Moll – you were fantastic! I didn't know you could dance like that.'

'There's still a lot you don't know about me, Hudson. I've always loved dancing and I've been practising on the quiet for a good few weeks now.'

'That's obvious, Moll – you were superb,' Ash smiled at her.

'You should win easily,' Hudson added, finding it very difficult not to stare at her studded navel.

'Hmm . . . maybe – you never know. But some of the older girls in Year 9 are pretty cool – it'll be interesting to see what they come up with.'

'And then there's me,' Ash said, taking off his top hat and placing it under his arm.

'What are you going to do in that get-up – the Funeral March?' Molly teased.

Ash dusted the top of his hat. 'Well, that's for me to know . . .'

'. . . and you to find out!' Hudson concluded. 'Now where have we heard that before?'

Molly giggled and slurped her drink.

The evening went on and the pupils of the Scrubs enjoyed themselves to the full.

The headteacher made a brief appearance, just to check up on things, and he even managed a faint smile as he walked around the hall. Hudson allowed himself to relax a little, but never too much – he knew he needed to keep his senses on full alert.

Bertie Small amazed everyone by winning the fancy dress competition – he smeared fake blood all over his hands and face, wore tattered clothes, dusted himself down with white flour and made an excellent job of looking like a decomposing corpse. He was so convincing that Miss Drew screamed when she saw him resting on the side of the stage – she thought he really was dead.

The other dance acts tried to outdo Molly's brilliant debut and a group of Year 9 boys did a brilliant take-off of a popular boy band – but everyone agreed that Molly would take some beating.

It was just after half-past nine when a flash of lightning lit up the windows on one side of the assembly hall, followed by a roar of thunder so loud that it was heard above the music. Hudson stopped dancing, grabbed Molly's arms and looked into her eyes. He saw in each one a reflected image of his own frightened expression.

He'd had no further warnings from GA, but Hudson suddenly sensed that things were about to take a strong turn for the worse.

And that was when he developed the most appalling headache . . .

17

The Final Curtain

At twenty minutes before ten Brinnie walked on to the stage, holding a glass of wine in one hand and a sausage roll in the other. Before he had a chance to speak, another dramatic bolt of lightning lit up the window to the left of the stage and everyone looked across. The ghoulish portraits grinned mockingly in the flashing light.

'Wow! These disco lights just get better every year,' Brinnie joked.

Again, a loud roar of thunder followed, shaking the foundations of the assembly hall and causing all the glass in the windows to rattle. A scowling pumpkin hanging from one of the ceiling lights began to swing.

'And this Hallowe'en is just getting spookier and spookier,' he added in a creepy voice.

The audience chuckled nervously.

Brinnie continued, 'OK, guys . . . Now it's time for the last of our six acts and we're going to change the tempo because young Ashley Swift of Year 7 is going to do a "Last Waltz" with a very special partner. And so without any further ado . . . it's over to him . . .'

The crowd pushed forward and the stage lights dimmed. Hudson and Molly fought their way to the front and Hudson noticed that the Mokee Joe figure had disappeared from the side of the stage.

And then Molly put her hands to her face and shrieked with laughter as Ash appeared holding the grotesque dummy in a passionate embrace and began dancing to the soothing music of a waltz.

Ash was still wearing his undertaker's outfit and the sight of him strutting around with his fake Mokee Joe towering above him had the audience in fits.

'Ash is brilliant,' Molly whispered to Hudson. 'It's his face – he looks so serious.'

Hudson tried to see the funny side, but his mind was really elsewhere. 'I know. I wish the real Mokee Joe could see this – just to see how ridiculous he looks.'

Ash carried on dancing, making perfect steps in time with his bizarre partner.

The audience shrieked with laughter.

And then another huge bolt of lightning lit up the windows. A few seconds later every light in the assembly hall went out, plunging the room into blackness.

The music petered out and just for a moment it went deathly quiet.

Someone in the audience made a spooky, howling noise and Bertie Small forgot he was a rotting corpse and started wailing.

'Hudson – what's happening?' Molly stammered, pulling at his arm.

But it was a familiar voice from the side of the stage that answered. 'Keep your heads, everybody.' Brinnie tried desperately to sound calm. 'I think the storm's knocked the power out – I'm sure it'll be back in a minute.'

'Are you OK, Ash?' Hudson shouted up from the gloom.

'Yes – fine!' Ash shouted back into the audience. 'But I can hardly see a thing up here.'

One of the vampire DJs, still backstage, managed to light a candle and Hudson could just about make out the shapes of Brinnie and Ash, still holding on to his 'partner'.

And then . . .

Molly screamed as she saw a familiar shape – a silhouette, at least seven feet tall – move out from the blackness at the back of the stage.

The vampire's candle went out.

'*Hudson, it was him. I saw him. He's up there.*'

The audience gasped as an almighty racket sounded from up on the stage. It sounded like some sort of huge animal running riot.

Somewhere among the chaos the audience heard Brinnie scream. Ash screamed. And then the audience screamed.

'Wait here – don't move,' Hudson said to Molly. He made his way over to the side of the hall and groped around until he found his briefcase. He opened it and felt for his big, rubber torch and then stumbled his way back.

But before he had the chance to switch it on, the power returned and the audience gaped at the scene on the stage.

Brinnie lay in a crumpled heap, clutching his arm. Even from down in the audience, Hudson could see it was badly broken. Ash stood in the middle of the stage with his arms by his side, stiff – like a statue – frozen in shock, but thankfully not hurt. The vampire at the back that had lit the candle had real blood trickling down his face from a deep gash on his forehead.

But by far the most alarming sight was that of the totally dismembered fake Mokee Joe. It had been savagely torn apart – its arms, legs and head all scattered to the far corners of the stage. The clothes were in shreds and the newspaper stuffing scattered everywhere.

The headteacher was the first to try and restore order. He appeared on stage looking white; his voice was trembling. 'Good Lord! Whatever happened? Is there an escaped animal in the hall?'

He took a mobile from his inside pocket and started phoning the emergency services.

Miss Drew followed on behind and took over. 'Does anyone have any idea what happened here?' she shouted into the audience.

Hudson looked up at her. 'Yes, miss – I do.'

Everything went quiet and all eyes turned and focused on the boy with the mysterious hairstyle, dressed like a small, mad professor, still clutching a big, rubber torch.

'Hudson!' Miss Drew exclaimed, full of surprise. 'Tell us then – what's happened here?'

But before he had a chance to answer, the lights went out again.

* * *

The monster had one big advantage over everyone, including Hudson. He could use his infrared vision and see in the dark.

Hudson just had time to switch on his torch, lighting up the hideous face as it charged towards him. Mokee Joe leapt down from the stage, trampling everyone in his way to get at his enemy.

'MOVE TO THE SIDES OF THE HALL!' Hudson screamed at the crowd.

It seemed a good idea – walls felt more secure – and a few moments later the floor was largely cleared as Mokee Joe closed in on his target.

The lights came back on again.

Nobody could believe their eyes at the sight that confronted them.

The terrifying seven-foot figure of Mokee Joe stood in the middle of the empty dance floor. An electric-blue light began to glow around him. As the realisation that this was not just another partygoer in disguise dawned on the spectators, shrieks and horrified gasps sounded around the hall.

Buggles, still on the stage, tried to exercise his authority. 'Now see here . . .'

Mokee Joe, glaring straight at Hudson, who had now moved with Molly to the edge of the dance floor, turned and faced the headteacher.

Buggles saw properly for the first time the black, piercing eyes, the ferocious expression under the angled eyebrows, the black-blue, tightly-drawn lips over the sharp fangs and the strange pock-marked blotches over the pallid skin . . .

'I-I don't know who you are . . . but I'm ph-phoning the police right now . . .' Buggles stammered, terror written all over his face.

He pressed the buttons on his mobile with trembling fingers as the demon stretched out one of his arms.

Hudson, Molly and everyone in the hall gasped with disbelief as an intense bolt of blue lightning flashed from the ends of the monster's long fingers, crackled through the air and struck the headteacher, causing him to scream and drop the phone.

This gave Hudson the precious few seconds he needed to decide what to do next. He turned, spotted the fire extinguisher on the wall and stepped towards it.

Before anyone knew what was happening, he ripped the safety device off its mounting and hurled it with deadly strength and accuracy at the gloating figure of his adversary.

The heavy red cylinder struck Mokee Joe full on the side of the head and knocked him flat.

Some of the crowd cheered, others gasped in horror as a loud CLANG resounded around the hall.

'Moll – go and pick up Buggles's phone and call the police – and an ambulance.'

Molly nodded and set off towards the stage just as Mokee Joe started to get up again.

'TONIGHT, WE SETTLE THIS ONCE AND FOR ALL!' Hudson called across to the monster – determined to keep its attention focused on himself.

But Mokee Joe seemed to understand that loyalty to one's friends can be as much a weakness as a strength. As Molly made for the stage, the evil fiend crouched and stretched out an arm again.

'MOLLY – WATCH OUT!' Hudson screamed. 'HE'S AIMING AT YOU!'

But the warning came too late. Hudson could only watch as she turned and saw the fingers release their charge. A horrible cracking, whipping sound filled the air as a second bolt of blue lightning struck Molly on the shoulder and knocked her to the ground.

Miss Drew, still on the stage standing by Ash, screamed and set off to help her.

But Mokee Joe moved more quickly. The monster ran towards Molly, scooped her limp body up under one arm and returned in triumph to the centre of the floor. Then the fiend screamed a high-pitched electronic scream that chilled the entire audience to the marrow before grinning the most evil grin back at his shocked adversary.

Hudson didn't know what to do. It seemed that his vile enemy had the upper hand.

He prayed that Guardian Angel would step in to help him.

That was when the emergency doors at the back of the assembly hall almost broke off their hinges.

'OK, EVERYBODY! STAY AS CALM AS YOU CAN AND KEEP TO THE SIDES OF THE HALL. JUST LEAVE THIS TO US. WE'LL SOON HAVE THE SITUATION UNDER CONTROL.'

The chief man in black lowered the loud-hailer and looked to his five companions by his side. Hudson recognised them as the six men who'd interviewed him in Buggles's study.

The crowd muttered in expectation, especially when, a few seconds later, a dozen special police, all armed with guns, filed into the back of the hall.

Hudson and the crowd looked over to Mokee Joe to see his reaction.

But the monster was no fool. With Molly, still unconscious, gripped under his arm, he knew he was safe from attack.

Hudson concentrated. At first, nothing – and then, at last, the voice.

'Climb the curtain at the side of the stage – make your way over to the silver sphere and hang above them . . . do it now!'

Whilst Hudson digested the message, the chief 'man in black' shouted from the back of the hall:

'DON'T ANYONE MOVE – KEEP STILL – ESPECIALLY THOSE ON THE STAGE.'

Buggles didn't need telling. He was frozen with shock, clutching his injured hand. Brinnie sat cross-legged, holding his broken arm, his face as white as a sheet. Miss Drew stood with her arm around Ash's shoulder trying to offer some kind of reassurance – though she looked as if she could have done with some herself. Mokee Joe gazed round at his shocked audience, his mind temporarily off Hudson, more intent on the gathering army mustering at the back.

This was the second vital distraction that Hudson needed.

As the monster looked towards the gunmen and took stock of the situation, Hudson gingerly made his way to the side of the stage until he was within reach of the black, trailing fabric. He disappeared behind it, gripped it as tight as he could and started hoisting himself upwards.

OK, GA – I'm on my way, he thought to himself.

At first, Hudson felt sure that the curtain material would tear, but if his strength had greatly increased, his weight had not, and it proved more than strong enough.

Up he went, his vice-like grip and surging biceps struggling against the almost impossible task. With all the determination he could muster he succeeded in climbing to a dizzy height and started making his way across the high ceiling towards centre stage.

Brinnie was the first to look up. Gripping the curtain tightly with one hand, Hudson put his index finger to his lips and gestured to the teacher to keep quiet. Brinnie got the message and looked away. Ash spotted him next and Hudson repeated the gesture.

A couple more metres and Hudson made his target. He reached out to the thick lighting flex hanging from the ceiling and lowered himself into a sitting position on top of the great silver sphere.

A huge gasp echoed around the assembly hall as the crowd spotted the small, mad professor sitting directly and comfortably above the monster's head.

It seemed the only pair of eyes in the entire room which did not know of Hudson's whereabouts belonged to Mokee Joe.

What next? Hudson thought to himself, beginning to feel strangely confident.

Before an answer could come through, the loudhailer at the back of the hall boomed out again:

'PUT THE CHILD DOWN, GENTLY – YOU'RE COMPLETELY SURROUNDED.'

Hudson looked down at poor Molly. Her eyes flickered and rolled back – she was beginning to regain consciousness as she wriggled under the creature's left arm. Her body arched back and the silver stud glistened in her navel.

Hudson felt angry and he was tempted to leap down on his enemy. But the voice in his head intervened:

'*No – take your friend from your pocket and use it as before.*'

Hudson needed no further explanation. He knew only too well how Mokee Joe was afraid of spiders, and now Spiffy might just be able to help him again – even though the arachnid had long since died.

Hudson sniggered to himself and quietly rummaged under his white lab coat into his jeans pocket. Yes, it was there – just as GA knew it would be.

Down below, Mokee Joe suddenly tuned in to Hudson's thought waves and looked up; but it was too late. The clear block of resin, containing Spiffy the ex-house spider, fell through the air and dropped with deadly accuracy. It landed neatly into the neck of Mokee Joe's grubby raincoat.

The monster, not realising what it was, dropped Molly to the floor and fumbled around with his free hand. A few seconds later he found it, plucked it out and held it in his energised palm.

The result was exactly as Hudson and GA predicted.

On seeing the huge, perfectly preserved, hairy spider changing colour through the clear plastic, the creature let out a shriek so shrill that everyone in the room's heart skipped a beat.

The monster leapt backwards. The crowd retreated tighter to the walls as Mokee Joe danced a frenzied dance – something between panic and rage.

This was the moment the 'men in black' had been waiting for. With Molly safely out of harm's way and the creature isolated in the middle of the dance floor . . .

'TAKE HIM!' the man with the loud-hailer blasted.

Guns were still out of the question – too many people around. Two policemen wearing helmets and wielding truncheons raced forward.

Hudson screamed down from his perch, 'NO! YOU DON'T KNOW WHAT YOU'RE DEALING WITH – STAY BACK!'

But it was too late.

As the men attacked and struck blows to Mokee Joe's steel-like frame, the monster grabbed them each by an arm and fired a powerful electric charge into their bodies. As they fell limp, he raised them up like toy soldiers and flung them back in the direction they'd charged from. Their bodies skidded across the shiny floor and stopped in a crumpled heap at the feet of the man with the loud-hailer. The two men lay there moaning – unable to comprehend what had happened.

It was too much for most of the crowd – they screamed in terror and shielded their eyes from the horror. Some ran from the hall, but most stayed rooted to the spot in complete shock.

Nobody quite knew what to do next as Mokee Joe turned and faced the stage, glowering up at his enemy.

But GA was already communicating the next move, though this time, Hudson had already worked it out for himself.

Using his body weight, he started to swing the ball from side to side like giant pendulum.

Molly was on her feet and almost recovered. She shouted up at him. 'Hudson! What are you doing? You'll kill yourself!'

'Trust me!' he shouted back, swinging ever higher.

The armed police at the back of the hall edged slowly forwards.

'STAY WHERE YOU ARE!' Hudson shouted to them. 'IT'S ME HE WANTS!'

He swung even higher, backwards and forwards, making a huge arc. The audience held its breath as the ceiling creaked loudly under the strain.

'DO YOUR WORST, FREAK . . .' Hudson yelled down at his enemy. 'WHAT ARE YOU WAITING FOR?'

Mokee Joe didn't hesitate.

He ran towards the stage, raised his bony hands and unleashed a mighty charge of crackling energy up at the moving target.

Hudson ducked behind the orb as the blue lightning struck the sphere and deflected on to the ceiling. A great shower of plaster rained down on to the floor, leaving a black hole burnt in the roof.

More screams from the audience – the gunmen moved closer and aimed their rifles.

'LEAVE HIM TO ME!' Hudson shouted at the small army again. 'I KNOW WHAT I'M DOING – HE'S ABOUT TO GET THE SHOCK OF HIS LIFE.'

Only GA knew what his protégé was up to – everyone else thought that the swinging mad professor had gone really mad.

Hudson looked down at his enemy and continued the process – calculating angles of incidence at lightning speed in his brain, calculating angles of deflection in relation to the degrees of arc of the swinging sphere on which he was sitting – his own thought waves combining with those of GA, his head becoming a super-computer that his mentor would be proud of . . .

And then, as the silver planet swung again through its dizzy orbit, Mokee Joe, now glowing more blue than ever before, took his final shot.

This time, the angle was exactly right – at least from Hudson's point of view.

A savage bolt of blue, snaking electricity struck the multi-faceted surface, but this time it reflected back exactly along the path it had arrived on – or almost.

As Mokee Joe sneered up at Hudson, the electric charge bounced back and struck him straight in his evil grinning face. The metal studs surrounding the face conducted the charge and hissed and crackled, sending the stunned creature reeling backwards, drawing all his own power back at him.

He screamed another chilling scream, his face still absorbing the piercing blue light.

Hudson watched his enemy's eyes roll backwards, arms waving helplessly in the air, the tall, gangly body racked in pain and falling helplessly out of control.

And then the alien body thudded on to the floor, not moving, the charge stopped – blue smoke rising from the grotesque head.

A deadly hush fell over the crowd.

The only sound was that of the light flex, creaking as it strained to support its heroic passenger up on the ceiling. And then the army rushed forward and overpowered the alien attacker before he had a chance to recover.

Finally, as it dawned on everyone that the boy with the strange hairstyle up on the glittering orb had somehow got the better of the demon intruder, the cheering started.

Hudson dropped down to the ground, landed on his feet with a great thud, jumped down from the stage and rushed over to Molly. Ash dashed over and joined them. The three friends looked at each other, said nothing, and hugged one another in relief.

Hudson glanced over at his enemy lying prostrate on the floor, the clear resin block by his side. He went over and picked it up and slid Spiffy carefully back into his pocket.

The pupils and staff of the Scrubs applauded and cheered louder than ever as the demon's body was carried out, wrapped in a straightjacket and tied with numerous ropes to a stretcher.

But Hudson's celebrations were cut short.

The voice in his head spoke up again.

'*The tall man in black is looking at you. Go with him – now. Don't ask any questions – just do as he says.*'

Hudson glanced around the spreading throng in front of the stage. Most of the officials had already melted away, but a number of policemen stood around the room taking statements from small groups of people, many still suffering the aftershock of the recent events. Blue lights flashed through the windows as police cars and ambulances waited outside.

But then Hudson turned round and looked up to the back of the stage and saw the figure standing there – just as GA had said – beckoning him towards the stage door.

'Over here . . .' the man in black said as quietly as possible.

Just for the minute, everyone on stage was too busy sorting out their own needs to notice anyone slipping away. Brinnie was having his arm looked at by a paramedic; Miss Drew was attending to the headteacher's burnt hand; other teachers were trying to clear the mess and re-establish some sort of order . . .

'Come on, you two – follow me,' Hudson whispered to Molly and Ash.

'Where to?' Molly asked, feeling she'd had quite enough excitement for one night.

'I can't be sure, but I've got a pretty good idea,' Hudson replied with a mysterious edge to his voice. 'And if I'm right then you'd never believe me anyway. Come on – we've got to move quickly.'

As Hudson led his two friends towards the man in black, he thought to himself, *And if I'm right, then the real show's only just started* . . .

18

Homeward Bound

Two black Daimlers stood just outside the school gates, their engines purring quietly. The tall man in black beckoned Hudson to get into the back seat of the car in front.

'Can my two friends come?' Hudson asked in a very calm voice.

The man went around the other side of the car and spoke to the driver through the window. He returned a few seconds later.

'OK – they can come too. Hop in the back seat.'

Whilst the man in black climbed into the front passenger seat, Molly and Ash followed Hudson into the back without question.

The man signalled to the driver and the car cruised

away from the playground, the second car following close behind.

'Hudson, *where are we going* – what's happening?' Molly and Ash whispered at the same time.

The man in black turned to face them.

'We're going to a place about ten minutes from here. Hudson has an important *rendezvous* to make.'

Hudson nodded. 'Guardian Angel – he's speaking to me now – telling me not to be afraid.'

Molly squeezed his arm. 'Do you know why he wants to meet up with you?'

'He's not telling me why just yet – he doesn't want to alarm me. But I've got a good idea what the reason is.'

'What?' Ash asked nervously. 'This sounds like something weird to me!'

Hudson didn't answer. He just stared ahead blankly, his hair bobbing up and down as the car turned down a bumpy track.

Ash whispered across to Molly, 'Hey . . . we're heading out to where we found the old church. Look – there's that overgrown pond.'

The car lurched on, the track becoming more overgrown and ever bumpier. The man in black jarred up and down in his seat and never spoke a word.

A few minutes later, the car juddered to a halt and the inside lit up with the headlights of the second car pulling up behind.

The driver spoke for the first time. 'We're here. Everybody out, and take care – it's dark and the track is full of potholes.'

Hudson snapped back to his senses and climbed out with Molly and Ash.

The rain had stopped and the temperature had dropped rapidly as the sky cleared. As the three friends stood shivering, still wearing their Hallowe'en outfits and feeling a little conspicuous to say the least, the man in black said something to the driver and sent him off.

A few minutes later the driver reappeared with three survival blankets and offered them around. Wrapping them around their shoulders, the three friends stood huddled together, feeling warmer, a little less tense, but at the same time very vulnerable.

All at once, Hudson looked up at the moon. Molly followed his gaze and stared at it, her mouth open. Ash did the same and gasped. The three men in black by their side, each holding a powerful torch, never even looked up.

'Is that amazing or what?' Ash exclaimed, his head still craned back.

Molly moved closer to Hudson and grabbed his arm. 'What's happening, Hudson? How come we can see the red spot without a telescope?'

'Because it's growing, and not only getting bigger – it's gaining in energy.'

Although Molly's face was in shadow, Hudson could see that she didn't really understand. He grabbed her hand and followed the three men with their torches.

From somewhere behind, three other men followed and two of them seemed to be carrying a stretcher.

As the strange night procession trampled through the rough undergrowth, a light sprang up in the distance, lighting up the treetops, and . . . a church steeple.

Molly was the first to spot one of the familiar leaning tombstones.

'It's the ruined church, Hudson, isn't it?'

'Yes, the church of St Michael de Rothchilde. It was built in 1654.'

'Wow! How did you know that?' Ash whispered.

'Guardian Angel still coming through?' Molly suggested.

'Exactly right,' Hudson confirmed, in a matter-of-fact way. 'He's waiting up there in that clearing – and he isn't alone.'

They passed the ruined church and suddenly the men in front didn't need their torches any more. The trees and shrubs shrank away to leave a large circular clearing, lit up with spotlights – with a big lorry parked in the centre and a huge crane standing by its side.

'My God! What's going on here?' Molly gasped.

'And what's on the back of that lorry?' Ash added. 'Why is it covered in tarpaulin?'

But before Hudson had a chance to reply, three more men came over towards them. The shorter one in the centre was very familiar.

Hudson trotted straight towards him – almost stretching his arms out to hug him.

'Guardian Angel! I can't believe all this is happening.'

Molly and Ash caught up and listened intently as the plump man with the enlarged head and kind eyes replied in a gentle voice:

'Don't be frightened Tor-3-ergon – it's your destiny. The mission has been completed and it's time for us to go back to our real home.'

Molly grabbed Hudson's arm and shook it. 'What does he mean, Hudson? What's all this about going home?'

Ash was distracted by the sound of a large engine. He watched as the crane lifted the large circular cargo off the back of the lorry and lowered it gently to the ground.

Hudson took no notice of it and stared deep into Molly's big brown eyes.

'I was only ever here to work with GA – to rid your planet of Mokee Joe.'

Hudson felt strange using language like 'your planet' and 'only ever here' and he could see by the look on Molly's face that she was very uncomfortable with it too.

'Move over, young lady, please,' one of the men in black suddenly requested.

The three friends stood to one side as two men walked past bearing a stretcher. By the looks on the men's faces, it was heavy and they didn't appear too happy about it.

'Mokee Joe,' GA said, reading the puzzled look on Ash and Molly's faces. 'He's harmless now, strapped up and ready for stowage on board.'

'Hey – you just said "on board". On board what?' Ash asked, full of wonder.

Hudson pointed over to the lorry's load, lying on the ground, just as the tarpaulin was being removed. 'That!'

Any sense of reality evaporated as the three friends found themselves staring at a large circular disc of shining metal. There appeared to be a windscreen of some sorts on the top surface and numerous air vents around its entire lower circumference.

It stood on three stout metal legs.

'This has just got to be a joke – that's the most unrealistic flying saucer I've ever seen!' Ash blurted out.

'You've got to agree, Hudson – it does look a bit of a prop,' Molly added, nervously.

Hudson looked at GA and they smiled at each other – a knowing kind of smile.

GA clasped his hands together and spoke again. 'And now we have to move on. I'm sorry but time is of the essence – the energy field will dissipate in less than six Earth hours.'

He looked at Ash and Molly's puzzled expressions and spoke more quickly. 'The red spot on the moon. It's an energy spot sent from Alcatron 3, our home planet. When we hover over it, the ship will totally absorb it and turn it into a massive burst of kinetic energy. It will literally blast us to just above the speed of light, back to the Plexus System – and then on to home.'

'Molly, this cannot be real – tell me this is all a dream,' Ash stammered, his mouth wide open.

But the tears welling up in Molly's eyes showed that she knew that this was all totally for real.

The party moved over towards the glistening ship, officials with clipboards crawling all over it like flies on a piece of meat. Many of the men wore white coats and thick spectacles – Hudson couldn't help thinking they looked very like the mad professor he was still dressed up as.

As they moved closer to the ship, more into the light, they saw that GA was wearing some sort of light blue boiler suit; his large head stood out in the bright lights and his enormous, kind eyes blinked with sharpness and intelligence.

'It is time to say your farewells to your Earth friends, Tor-3-ergon.'

Hudson turned to Ash and took his hand in a firm handshake.

'Stay cool, Ash. Take care and look after yourself. Have a great life and take this. It'll help you to remember

Hudson reached in his pocket and took out the clear resin block containing Spiffy.

Ash almost choked as he took it. He knew how valuable it was to his friend.

'Thanks,' Ash whispered, his voice trembling. 'You stay cool too, and keep yourself safe from monsters and things.'

Hudson watched as Ash looked down at the ground. It was obvious his friend didn't know what else to say.

Molly began to cry quietly. Hudson had never seen his best friend cry before – it shocked him. He took a deep breath and took hold of her hands.

'Moll . . . I . . . I . . . don't know what to say,' Hudson stuttered, a big lump forming in his throat.

Ash disappeared into the background and left the two best friends facing each other with arms outstretched.

'I can't believe I won't see you again,' Molly sobbed. 'It's not as if you're going to come back – it's more like you're going to die or something. Don't go, Hudson.'

At that moment, Molly had never looked more vulnerable, her eyes leaking big tears, running down her cheeks in small streams. Her small tough body that had caught out Mokee Joe so many times now shook and trembled.

It was a side to Molly that Hudson had never seen before and it made him want to hold her tight and keep her with him.

And then Hudson read her mind and knew that Molly felt the same – she never wanted to leave him – ever!

The body of Mokee Joe, still limp, had been loaded on to the ship. GA offered to show the body to Hudson, explaining that it had been secured by steel strapping and was damaged, de-energised and quite harmless. But Hudson declined. He said he'd seen enough of Mokee Joe for the time being and would take GA's word for it.

Several government scientists came on board and Hudson overheard them talking about lines of magnetic force. It seemed that the churchyard lay directly over a large concentration of magnetic ore – lodestone. This had provided Mokee Joe with much of his energy source. Overhead cables and electricity pylons surrounding the marsh, as well as the nearby magnet factory, had also played their part in providing the Mokee Man with enormous power.

Finally, after much more coming and going, the government officials retreated, some still taking photographs, some still taking notes. The lorry and crane had long since gone and the surrounding spotlights were dimmed.

GA and Hudson stood alone at the controls.

A steady hum issued from the craft.

It was a sound like no other – a soft vibrating pulse that caused roosting birds to scatter from the trees, their dark silhouettes spiralling upwards to the crystal clear moon, the red spot still visible against its cratered yellow face.

The hum increased in volume and intensity. The three metal legs retracted into the bottom of the craft as it powered itself to hover above the marshy ground.

GA clicked the controls with nimble fingers, his brain working at incredible speed, calculating, estimating, and then the silver disc lifted towards the night sky, slowly at first, poised and full of purpose. The small crowd below shielded their eyes as a dazzling glow spread around the base of the ship.

And then it accelerated upwards so quickly that, within seconds, it was only visible as a distant moving light in the night sky – like an aeroplane at high altitude, but with a long trail, like a shooting star.

And then it was gone.

Down below, a small figure, still wrapped in a blanket, stood next to the chief man in black, staring in wonder into the night sky, until a car pulled up by their side, beckoned them in and drove slowly away. The small army of government officials and special police moved quickly off the site and within minutes, the clearing was deserted, devoid of any activity – as if nothing had ever happened there.

Epilogue

As midnight arrived on the strangest of Hallowe'en nights, a second cloudbank moved in across Danvers Green and the night became darker and more suited to witches and broomsticks – only the moon resisted the clouds and shone bright in the eastern sky.

A cold wind whipped up, snaking amongst the old tombstones of St Michael de Rothchilde, moaning eerily through the ruins of the old church. Withered leaves scurried across the stone flagged floor and startled a lone bat, which spiralled up into one of the ancient naves and settled in the corner of an arched window. This window was high and secluded and had largely escaped the attention of trespassers and vandals. Apart from a small hole in the top right-hand corner, the original stained glass panel was still intact.

It showed a large Gothic figure dressed in sackcloth, a hood draped over its head, and beneath the cowl a ghoulish face – skeletal, with piercing eyes and a fearsome grin. And at the feet of the demon, two children fleeing in terror. Beside the chilling image, a date was engraved on the glass – 1793.

And now, through the hole where the glass had been broken, it was possible to see a small dot of light, high in the night sky, moving closer towards a pulsating red spot on the moon.

The government scientists tracked the ship easily.

They followed its progress as it moved into lunar orbit, just one hour and eleven minutes since take-off. After orbiting the moon twice, they watched as the ship altered course and moved in on the pulsating red spot, hovering directly above it.

And then at thirteen minutes past midnight, both the ship and the spot totally disappeared.

Meanwhile, down on Earth, a lonely light shone from the sitting-room window of number 13, Tennyson Road. Whilst Mr Brown snored loudly from upstairs, Mrs Brown sat in her armchair and clicked away with her knitting needles, faster than ever. She sobbed quietly and looked at the cup of cold chocolate sitting on the table by her side. Pugwash walked over, rubbed against her legs and looked up at her with sad eyes.

Apart from the demon cargo, the ship's occupants were all changed into their special silver suits and suspended in a deep sleep. Over by the control panel, a light blue boiler suit, a small white lab coat and a crimson crop-top lay amongst a pile of clothes arranged on one of the empty seats.

As the automatic pilot steered the ship on its homeward course, Hudson dreamed his favourite dreams – of red skies, green beaches and crimson sunsets; gentle waves lapping on to the shore, caressing his feet as he walked barefoot through the soft sand; and of Molly, by his side, smiling at him.

Mokee Joe lay totally helpless, defeated for the second time. Only the tiniest flicker of life remained in his burnt-out circuits. But it was still sufficient for the abominable terminator to detect the colossal magnetic field that was rapidly approaching the ill-fated ship and its totally unsuspecting crew . . .

ACKNOWLEDGEMENTS

I firmly believe that the initial success of *Mokee Joe is Coming!* and its excellent prospects, along with *Mokee Joe Recharged*, is due to the initial enthusiasm and sustained commitment of a dedicated team of individuals, namely:

Odette Bride, Dot Morritt, Hayley Barker, Joanne Hodgkinson, Anne Finnis, Anne McNeil and the Hodder team, Eve White, and of course, my wife and immediate family.